*"I didn't ask you to kiss me. I told you to kiss me,"* Maddie said wickedly

Austin shook his head. "You used to be so...nice."

"Nice girls finish last." She sized him up. "You've changed, too. The bad boy I once knew wouldn't turn down a kiss with a willing woman."

His eyes suddenly gleamed with challenge and something dark and delicious and forbidden. "Who says I've turned it down?" Then he was pressing his lips to hers. The kiss was hot and insistent, his mouth plundering hers. But just when she was really getting into it, he drew back.

"You asked for a kiss—there you go. Objective achieved."

But her objective had changed, Maddie realized. She was no longer the awkward seventeen-year-old who'd fantasized about kissing the cutest boy in high school. She was all grown up now and her fantasies went way beyond a kiss.

"Not quite."

"What else do you want from me?"

She licked her lips and stared into his eyes. "You and me...and some down and dirty, hot and heavy *sex.*"

# Blaze™

Dear Reader,

My heroes have always been bad boys! Nothing could be better than seeing a wild, wicked, dangerously handsome man who's too big for his britches humbled by the overwhelming power of love. Then again, if that man is one of a trio of notorious bad boy brothers from Cadillac, Texas, then you're talking triple the fun and the *blazing*-hot excitement!

Thanks to the overwhelming reader response to Dallas Jericho, the youngest brother featured in "Show & Tell" from the Blaze Midnight Fantasies anthology, I'm back this month with another hot, hunky, badder-than-bad Jericho brother in *The Sex Solution*. Austin is the oldest and wildest of the three, but he's determined to change his ways. No more fast times and fast women. He's a new man, and to prove it, he intends to find a nice, conservative, *tame* woman to settle down with. But when former good girl Madeline Hale rolls back into town with seduction on her mind, she soon convinces him that being a little bad can be very, *very* good!

I love writing hot, steamy love stories that portray not only the emotional bond between a man and woman, but the physical bond, as well. Blaze gives me the freedom to do just that. So grab an ice-cold drink, crank up the air-conditioning and get ready for a red-hot read from deep in the heart of Texas!

All my best,

*Kimberly Raye*

P. S. There's still one Jericho brother who's footloose and fancy free. But not for long. Don't miss the final showdown in Blaze #131, *The Fantasy Factor,* coming next month.

# THE SEX SOLUTION
## *Kimberly Raye*

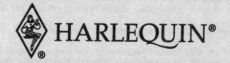

HARLEQUIN®

TORONTO • NEW YORK • LONDON
AMSTERDAM • PARIS • SYDNEY • HAMBURG
STOCKHOLM • ATHENS • TOKYO • MILAN • MADRID
PRAGUE • WARSAW • BUDAPEST • AUCKLAND

This book is dedicated to the real Marshalyn Simmons
aka Sue Groff.
You're the best mother-in-law in the world,
and an even better friend!

ISBN 0-373-79131-3

THE SEX SOLUTION

Copyright © 2004 by Kimberly Groff.

This edition published by arrangement with Harlequin Books S.A.

Visit us at www.eHarlequin.com

**Printed in U.S.A.**

# *1*

---

EVERYTHING ABOUT HIM promised hot, steamy, *mind-blowing* sex.

From the way he looked…

So rugged and masculine with his white cotton T-shirt, the words *Cowboy Up* emblazoned in black letters across the front. Perspiration soaked the material, making it nearly transparent. Dark swirls of hair covered his broad chest. Damp cotton clung to his shoulders and biceps. Soft, faded denim cupped his crotch and molded to trim hips and long, muscular legs, the cuffs tucked into a pair of dusty brown cowboy boots.

To the way he moved…

So strong and sure and purposeful as he reached for a sack of feed on the hot pavement near his feet. Muscles rippled and flexed as he hoisted the weight onto his shoulder. One hair-dusted thigh played peekaboo with her through a frayed rip in his jeans as he turned and tossed the load into the bed of a beat-up pickup truck.

Definitely *mind-blowing*. A man as strong and toned and blatantly physical as Austin Jericho would never be a lazy lover. He would touch and stroke and stir a woman until she screamed for release.

Not that Madeline Regina Hale knew such a thing firsthand. Only in her most private, provocative dreams.

She stared through the glass of Skeeter's Drugstore and tried to calm the sudden pounding of her heart. Even after twelve years, Austin was still the hottest boy in Cadillac, Texas.

Make that the hottest *man*. One-hundred percent, prime, Grade-A, pinch-me-I'm-dreaming *man*.

Her breath caught at another squat, another flash of hard, muscular thigh.

The reaction sent a rush of nostalgia through her and suddenly all those years, a challenging career as the senior research-and-development chemist for one of America's leading cosmetics companies and a shelf full of well-read self-improvement books didn't seem to matter.

Madeline felt seventeen again. Young. Naive. Awkward. And lovesick over a hot teenage boy in dusty boots and a black leather Harley jacket.

Back then he'd looked every bit as delicious as he did right now. His jeans had been just as flattering, and her heart had fluttered just as much.

She'd always had a powerful physical reaction to Austin.

He, on the other hand, had never had any reaction to her.

She couldn't really blame him. She'd been practically nonexistent back then. Just another geeky, four-eyed member of the Chem Gems—the only academic club at a school that lived and breathed football and state championships. Forget victory parties with the *in* crowd. She'd spent her Saturday nights in the kitchen of her dad's doughnut shop, Sweet & Simple, mixing up muffins and fritters and other goodies for the Sunday-morning rush. The expected pastime of the overweight wallflower voted Most Studious for four consecutive years.

Austin, on the other hand, had been lean, loud and rebellious. The oldest of the notorious Jericho brothers—a hot, handsome trio of heartbreakers who'd invented the word *scandal*. A leather-clad bad boy who'd ridden a screaming chrome demon and shot every rule to hell and back. The boy voted Most Likely to Serve Time in a Maximum Security Prison.

Dangerous. That had been Austin way back when.

His attitude. His looks. His effect on the opposite sex.

Only a select few females had been lucky enough to keep company with him, however. Most had been blond and beautiful, with big boobs and even bigger egos. All had been as wild as the boy himself.

Mousy-brown hair, a chubby figure—thanks to all those Saturday nights at the bakeshop—and a humdrum existence had knocked Madeline completely out of the running. She'd had to settle for lusting after him from afar.

Then and now.

As soon as the thought struck, she stiffened. While she was, indeed, staring and lusting from a substantial distance, things *had* changed.

She'd changed.

Expensive blond highlights, a strict diet-and-exercise regime, makeup lessons and subscriptions to

*Cosmopolitan* and *Vogue* had seen to that. But even more, she'd evolved on the inside, as well as the outside. She no longer settled for what life doled out. She didn't sit around waiting for luck or the right moment or perfect alignment of the planets to experience what life had to offer. She went after what she wanted when she wanted it. She didn't content herself with dreams. She *made* things happen, and she lived for every exciting moment.

Her cell phone chose that moment to shriek, drawing her attention away from the sweaty, succulent picture of Austin to the overflowing leather sack she called a purse.

"Girlfriend, where *are* you?" Janice demanded. Janice was the ex-vice president of the Chem Gems and the maid of honor for Cheryl Louise Martin's wedding—the reason Madeline had taken time off from her job at V.A.M.P. Cosmetics to make the hundred-and-fifty-mile drive from Dallas to her small hometown.

Cheryl Louise, two years Maddie's junior, had been an honorary Chem Gem thanks to her older sister, Sharon, who'd let her tag along to study group. Their parents had been busy running Chester's Diner—the family business—and so Sharon had been in charge of her little sister while her dad cooked and her mom waited tables. Since the Chem Gems—all five of them—had been best friends as well as study partners, they'd all taken charge of Cheryl, particularly Madeline. She and Sharon had been best friends since kindergarten.

*Had.*

An image rushed at her. Of a dark night and a deadly curve and a monstrous tree and...

Madeline closed her mind to the memory the way she always did. Sharon's death was in the past and dwelling on that night wasn't going to bring her friend back.

Besides, Sharon wouldn't want tears ruining the occasion. She would want her little sister to have a grand send-off. Exactly what the Chem Gems intended to give her.

Starting with the bachelorette party tonight.

"He-llo?" Janice's impatient voice drifted over the line. "Girl, you were supposed to be here ten minutes ago to hang crepe paper for the pre-party festivities."

"I'm at Skeeter's getting everything on the list you dictated over the phone to me last night." Her gaze drifted back to the window in time to see Austin hoist the last sack of feed, pull off his gloves and stuff them into his back pocket. How he fit anything back there was a puzzle for Einstein himself.

"...get the extra batteries for Sarah's camera?" The tail end of Janice's question pushed past the pounding of Madeline's heart.

She forced a deep breath and shifted her attention to her basket. "Got 'em."

"How about the extra rolls of film?"

"Got 'em." She had to get control of herself. She wasn't seventeen anymore and Austin Jericho wasn't all that. He was just a man. Just flesh and blood. Just tanned skin and bulging muscle.

The thought drew a quick image from one of her favorite Austin fantasies.

*He gripped the hem of his T-shirt. Material bunched
and crept up his rock-hard abdomen and broad chest,
until he pulled the soft cotton over his head and tossed
it aside. Tanned fingers went to the button on his snug
jeans. The edges sagged with relief as the fastening
slid free. A zipper hissed and parted and...*

Madeline derailed the thought before she went
around the curve into The Land of the Sexually Deprived.

That was the problem.

Over the past six months, she'd been so fixated on
developing a new body lotion for V.A.M.P. that her
personal life had fallen by the wayside. She hadn't
been out on a Saturday night since the project's start.
She was bound to go a little bonkers when faced with
a hot, sweaty cowboy.

Particularly *this* hot, sweaty cowboy who'd domi-
nated her adolescent fantasies, and a few of her adult
ones, as well.

"...there? Earth to Madeline?" Janice huffed.
"Girlfriend, what is *with* you?"

"I'm tired, that's all. I just drove in this morning."

"You'll have plenty of time to rest after tomorrow."

Two weeks to be exact. Madeline had vetoed buying a bread maker for a wedding present and, instead,
had promised to house-sit for Cheryl while she hon-
eymooned in the Bahamas. Madeline would have
bought the appliance, but hearing the young woman
fret over who was going to take care of her plants and
her dog had been too much. Madeline didn't do guilt
very well, so she'd volunteered.

Besides, when she worked on a project, she preferred solitude. No colleagues interrupting her, no higher-ups chomping at the bit for a hint about what she was doing, no marketing personnel bugging her about deadlines. This way, everyone would be miles away and she could concentrate.

Not that she didn't like the big city and its noise and chaos. And its traffic. And its smog. And its endless miles of concrete. She loved it all. That's why she'd left Cadillac in the first place.

At least that's what Madeline had told herself for the past twelve years. So often, in fact, that she'd actually started to believe it.

"Don't forget the balloons. They have balloons, don't they? I've gotten used to a Wal-Mart on every corner. Cadillac could take some lessons from Houston."

"Some people like a slower pace." What was she saying? *The truth,* a voice whispered. *Some people do like a slower pace.*

Madeline just wasn't one of them. Was she?

"And there are people who pierce major body parts, too, but that doesn't mean they're sane." Janice's voice took on her familiar I-want-everything-to-go-perfectly desperation. "Please tell me they have balloons."

"I'm about to find out." Madeline headed down one of the aisles, passed a variety of cookies in favor of a large package of Double Stuffed Oreos. Otherwise known as inspiration. Whenever she came up against a brick wall at work, she would indulge in Oreos and free her creativity.

With the wedding looming and a size-ten brides-maid's dress to squeeze herself into, she'd been Oreo-free for the past few weeks, so she'd yet to come up with any really great ideas. She had a few so-so ones, but nothing outstanding. Or revolutionary. Nothing guaranteed to wow the CEO of V.A.M.P. and move Madeline the final step up the corporate ladder to head of research and development.

Yet.

With the aroma of chocolate wafers and sweet cream filling her nostrils and blessed solitude helping her focus, she would surely come up with something brilliant. Then it was back to Dallas and constant interruptions and her strict diet regime that consisted of Melba toast, grilled chicken salads and Pilates.

"Okay, we've hit pay dirt on the balloons," she told Janice a few seconds later.

"And hats? Do they have hats, too?"

"It's a bachelorette party, not a birthday party."

"Hats are festive. I want everyone in the party mood. I want tonight to be special."

"We'll all be together for the first time in twelve years. It'll be special."

"Except that Cheryl Louise is bringing her poodle, Tilly. Remember? She's the one that farts when she wags her tail. *Every* time she wags her tail."

"We'll make the best of it. Focus on the positive."

Madeline had learned that all-important lesson when she'd left Cadillac and headed for the big city. One of her first life-changing vows had been to stop stressing over the fact that she wasn't thin enough or pretty enough or outgoing enough, and *do* something about it.

She'd done just that and changed her life forever.

"Girl, you're absolutely right. She may be bringing Tilly, but at least she's leaving Twinkles at home," Janice sighed. "Otherwise, we'd all end up covered in dog hair. That blasted thing sheds like—ohmigod! Peanuts!" she shrieked. "You can't forget the peanuts. Cheryl loves peanuts and I want to have all of her favorites tonight."

"Got 'em." So much for a pep talk. "See you in a little while." No sooner had she punched off the off button than the phone rang again.

"A black laundry marker," Janice quipped. "Do they have one?"

"Skeeter's has everything."

It was the typical old-time drugstore that carried everything from small hardware items to makeup, canned goods to candy. They even had a pharmacy in the back where Ben Skeeter had been filling prescriptions for as long as Madeline could remember.

"Good. Now hurry up. Sarah just got here with the cheese dip."

"Yes, ma'am." She dropped the phone into her purse.

A few minutes later, after retrieving the requested marker, she headed for the pharmacy counter at the rear of the store where a silver-haired woman hoisted a large box onto the counter next to the cash register.

"Maddie Hale?" Camille Skeeter pushed her wire-framed glasses up onto her nose for a better look. "My word, is that you?"

"It's me, all right. *Madeline* Hale." She'd left the name Maddie behind with her geeky image.

The older woman smiled as she yanked open the box and reached for her pricing gun. "My, my, you're a sight. I wish Ben were here to see you, but he's over at the community center leading the dedication for the new monkey bars." She tapped the button pinned to her white smock.

Ben Skeeter's image stared back at Madeline along with the phrase printed around the edges that read *Ain't Nothin' Sweeter Than Electin' a Skeeter.*

"Ben's the mayor now," Camille told her. "Second term."

"I heard through the grapevine. Congratulations. So, are you handling the store all by yourself now?"

"Sure am." Camille wiped the sweat from her brow, hoisted the box to the side and reached for Madeline's basket. "But a woman's gotta do what a woman's gotta do and I always stand by my man. So—" she started ringing up items "—how are your mama and daddy doing? Haven't heard much from them since they retired down south. How do they like Port Aransas?"

"They were a little bored at first, but they've fallen into a nice routine. Dad spends his days fishing and doing his best to steer clear of anything that even smells like a doughnut. Mom opened a seashell shop."

"Sounds like they're having a ball."

"Finally." Her mother had spent twenty years as a high-school science teacher while her father had run the local doughnut shop. Her mother had been an academic, content to study life rather than really live it, while her father had been a workaholic who'd observed it from behind a counter.

Until last year.

Her mother's diagnosis with chronic heart disease had helped them realize what Madeline herself had learned that fateful day she'd lost Sharon—life was simply too short to waste. They'd sold their house and the doughnut shop and headed for the Texas coast.

"Mom's making conch-shell necklaces and Dad's catching giant redfish." And Madeline had a full jewelry box and an overflowing freezer to prove it. "They're really into this new phase of their lives."

"That's because it's fun. Ben and I need more fun in our lives, but his schedule is so demanding and the store needs me practically twenty-four/seven." She sighed, then smiled. "What about you, sweetie? I hear you're working for one of those fancy cosmetic companies up in Dallas."

"V.A.M.P. Cosmetics." Madeline rummaged in her bag. "Here are some samples of our new berry-flavored lipsticks."

Camille dabbed on the color and licked her lips. "My, my, but this tastes good. Whewee! My taste buds are in overload. I bet Ben will love it. He hates the brand I wear now. Says it tastes like wax."

Marketing objective accomplished.

V.A.M.P. Cosmetics had grown from a small business to a major corporation by focusing on the sensual nature of their products. They had lotions that tingled when applied. Mascara that made even the skimpiest lashes look lush and sexy. Bath gel that smoothed over the skin like a lover's silky touch. And lipsticks to spice up every kiss. *Seduce your senses.* That was V.A.M.P.'s creed.

"So is it true that you actually mix all this stuff up yourself?" Camille asked as she started to bag Maddie's purchases.

"I sure do."

"Amazing."

"I suppose so." Considering the only thing Madeline had mixed up way back when had been batches of muffins and glazed fritters in the kitchen of her dad's shop.

"So what are you cooking up right now?" The woman's eyes lit. "Is it a new lipstick? Why, I'm just a sucker for lipstick."

"Actually, my next project will be for our skin-care line. I don't know very many details yet—it's still in the developmental stage—but when I get something mixed up, I'll drop by a few samples."

"Would you? Oh, I would love that!" Camille slid the mini lipsticks into her coat pocket and stifled a cough. "Excuse me, sweetie. I just can't seem to get rid of this danged old croup." She reached behind the counter for a glass of water. After taking a sip, she cleared her throat and smiled. "So what else can I get for you today?"

Madeline glanced past the woman to the condom display and pointed to an extralarge blue box. "I'll take a pack of those."

"Sweet *and* smart." Camille winked and rang up the last item.

"More like afraid." At Camille's questioning glance, Madeline added, "We're decorating for Cheryl's bachelorette party. If I show up without the condoms, Janice will tar and feather me. She's a little obsessive.''

After paying for her purchases, Madeline gathered up her bag of goodies and started for the front of the store. She'd made it two steps before her cell phone rang again. She shifted her bag to one arm and rummaged inside her purse for the blasted phone.

"Trojan," Janice said the moment Madeline managed to say hello.

"Got 'em," Madeline rounded the corner. "Would you please stop worry—hmmph!''

Her breath caught as she came up hard against a solid mass of warmth. Her heart stalled. Her phone took a dive for the floor. Her purse hit with a solid thunk. Her bag crashed and the contents scattered.

"I'm so sorry," she started. "I didn't see—''

*You* lodged behind the sudden lump that blocked her throat. Her head jerked up and she found herself standing chest to chest with Cadillac's most notorious bad boy.

# 2

AUSTIN JERICHO'S EYES were even bluer than Maddie remembered. Deeper. More unnerving.

They pulled her in and sucked her under like a cool river on a hot summer's day. Sensation washed over her body, skimming her ultrasensitive skin, sneaking into every hot spot until she felt completely submerged and temporarily paralyzed and...*ahh.*

"I thought I recognized you." His voice, so rich and husky, slid into her ears and prickled the hair on the nape of her neck. Her attention shifted to his mouth.

He'd always had great lips. Slightly full on the bottom. Sensuous. Just right for kissing, or so she'd thought every time he'd folded himself into the desk opposite hers and opened his book for their daily algebra les—

"You recognized me?" she blurted as his words registered. "You recognized *me?*" Sure, they'd spent every afternoon together for most of their senior year, thanks to Marshalyn Simmons, the high-school librarian, who'd recruited Madeline to tutor Austin. But otherwise, he'd barely acknowledged her existence.

Except once.

Standing in the shadows outside the football stadium on a Friday night when the Cadillac Coyotes had been slaying the Hondo Hogs in a record-breaking game. The first and last football game Madeline Hale had ever attended.

She'd given up her usual Saturday night at the doughnut shop in favor of the chance to see Austin somewhere other than the school library. Not that it had been a date or anything like that. Just a chance meeting that she'd taken great pains to plan. They'd happened into each other near the concession stand.

She could still smell the fresh buttered popcorn and hear the roar of the crowd and feel the wild air emanating from the boy who'd walked up to her. He'd stared down into her eyes and she'd stared up into his, and they'd had nothing short of explosive chemistry.

For a few precious seconds.

But then the moment of truth had come and she'd learned one of life's biggest lessons—geeky good girls like Maddie did *not* end up with cool bad boys like Austin. She wasn't brave enough, bold enough, *bad* enough.

Then again, she wasn't plain old Maddie anymore. She was Madeline Hale. Sophisticated. Worldly. *Bad.*

But with Austin so close and overwhelming and still sexy as hell, it was hard to remember that.

"When I spotted you through the window," he told her, "I said to myself, 'Why, that looks like Maddie Hale' and sure enough—" he gestured to her "—here you are."

"You saw me through the window? *You* saw *me?*" Even as the question passed her lips, she knew she should bite it back and think of something witty to say. But it was hard to think with his heat surrounding her.

And his scent filling her nostrils…the musky smell of horse and leather and warm male that made her drink in a deep breath.

And his smile right there, directed at her…

As if he read the thoughts racing through her mind, his lips parted, his grin widened and her heart stalled.

Yep, that smile could do enough damage all by itself. Add it to everything else wreaking havoc on her senses and she was a lost cause.

"You saw me," she said again, as if repeating the truth would help it to sink in. "*You* saw *me*."

"You look really good."

"*I* look *good?*" She shook her head. *Goober alert!* "I mean, uh, yes, I do look rather good." *Conceited goober alert!* "Um, so do you. Look good, that is. You look really good."

"I look more wet than anything else. It's hot enough to fry eggs outside." He glanced down and plucked at his damp T-shirt. "But thanks anyway."

"Even all dusty and sweaty you look really good," she rushed on. "*Especially* all dusty and sweaty."

He grinned again. "I could use something cold to drink. Say—" he looked at her as if an idea had just struck "—maybe we could grab a root beer float over at the fountain. I mean, if you're not busy."

"You want to have a float? With me?" *Here comes the goober again.* "I mean, of course you want to have a float with me. I like floats. I mean, I used to like floats. I stick to diet sodas now."

"Diet soda?" He gave her a puzzled look as he

studied her. "Are you okay? You didn't hit your head or anything when we collided, did you?"

"I…" Boy, he smelled good. And felt good. And looked good.

She found herself wishing that she'd worn her black slacks. Black was slimming and her thighs needed all the help they could get.

The thought drew her up short and she stiffened. "I'm okay." She was, and she didn't need black slacks to prove it. *Mind over matter,* she told herself, and her mind was much bigger than her matter, even if she'd barely managed to squeeze said matter into the size-ten jeans hugging her thighs. She was no longer fat. She was voluptuous. And proud of every inch. "I'm fine, really."

"That's good news." He shifted his attention away from her then, thank goodness, and glanced around them.

Reality zapped her and she followed his gaze to the spilled contents of her bag. "That's what I get for being in a hurry." She dropped to her knees, grateful for a distraction from Austin and the all-important fact that he was standing just inches away from her.

She forced the notion aside and concentrated on gathering up her stuff. "They don't make bags like they used to…." Her words faded as her attention snagged on the worn tips of his boots.

Boots were good. Totally nonsexual. They shouldn't inspire lewd thoughts. Unless, of course, they drew to mind a vision of him so strong and powerful and naked, except for the boots….

Her nipples tingled. Her thighs trembled. And she felt dampness between her legs.

She drew a deep breath and reached for a canister of peanuts with one hand and a pack of batteries with the other.

"Good choice."

"Thanks. You can recharge these if you want..." Her words faded as she realized he wasn't talking about the pack of AA's, but the box of Trojans he'd retrieved.

Embarrassment flooded her. "Those aren't—" she started but then her eyes collided with his.

Hunger.

There was no mistaking the sudden flash in his deep blue stare. For several fast, furious heartbeats, she was seventeen all over again, staring at him over an open algebra book, wanting him and wishing that he wanted her the way he wanted the blueberry muffin she'd brought for him that day.

But this was no daydream. And there was no blueberry muffin. He was looking back at her now, and he wanted her just as much. It was right there in his eyes. In the way his gaze hooked on her lips...

"You always invest in such a big box?"

"They're not—" she started before common sense kicked in and she bit her tongue. "Um, bigger is always better."

A sexy grin tugged at his lips. "And here I thought size wasn't a big issue with women."

"Small is okay, but big is more economical. You get more bang for your buck." Heat crept up her neck and she drew in a steady breath. "Especially with this brand. They give you three free.'' Okay, she'd wandered into the land of goober again. Here she was discussing condoms with Austin Jericho.

"I've always bought the red pack myself, but maybe I'll give these a try."

"They're much better." As if she knew. "Better value and they're, um—" she glanced at the colorful package "—lubricated."

He nodded. "Lubrication's good."

"And they have spermicide. You've got to have that."

"Absolutely."

"So what were you saying about us having a—"

"I've really got to go," he cut in, his expression abruptly closing as if he'd just remembered something vitally important. He stuffed the condoms into her bag and pushed to his feet.

Madeline gathered up the last of her stuff and stood. Had she heard him wrong? "But what about that diet cola?"

"Can't stomach the stuff myself. Too much aftertaste."

"You can have a float and I'll have the diet cola."

"I'd love to, darlin', but I've got a sick horse waiting." He retrieved a written prescription from his pocket. "The vet says I need some of Ben's liniment." He handed the sack to her. "Here you go. Nice to see you again, Maddie."

"It's Madeline. No one really calls me Maddie anymore."

Surprise flashed in his eyes again as he watched her for a few fast, furious heartbeats. "Madeline," he finally repeated, a frown on his face, as if the name left a bad taste in his mouth. "Take care." And then he strode toward the pharmacy counter, leaving her to wonder what had just happened.

First off, he'd actually *noticed* her and—*ring!*

Her thoughts were dissolved by the shrill sound of her cell phone. Madeline tore her attention from Austin's delectable backside and turned to her oversize purse.

"I'm walking out the door right now," she told a frantic Janice when she finally managed to answer.

She swallowed a sudden thirst for diet cola, gathered up her purchases and headed out to her black Mustang waiting at the curb. The phone rang again as she climbed behind the wheel.

"Girl, we need ice," Janice quipped.

"Ice," Madeline said, and stabbed the off button.

She was barely able to ignore the urge to kill the power completely. She was irritated, not irresponsible. She knew Duane, her lab assistant, might need her.

A wave of anxiety went through her as she thought of the young man. She turned on the car, flicked the air conditioner on high and quickly punched in the familiar number.

Duane was a maverick—fresh and creative, and not much for following rules. That's what made him so brilliant. He wasn't afraid to try new things. To take chances. Unfortunately, fearlessness equaled carelessness sometimes.

Madeline stifled a nervous flutter. She'd taken time off before, albeit only a few days, and her lab had still been standing when she'd returned. Of course, her desk had been a little charred around the edges after Duane had ignored the no-food rule and chowed down on a chili dog while mixing up a new acidic skin peel just inches away. Unfortunately, the chili had contained several spices that, when mixed with some of the acid compounds, proved combustible.

"Are you okay?" she demanded when he picked up the phone after the tenth ring.

"I'm not even eating chili today. But, man oh man, I could use a good cup of coffee. And a peanut-butter sandwich."

She did a mental evaluation of the ingredients of both, and tried to pinpoint any contrary elements. Nothing. Still, she wasn't taking any chances. "Eat in the break room."

"Don't I always?"

"Actually—" she started.

He rushed on. "I've turned over a new leaf. I'm a new man. Walking around without eyebrows for six months will do that to a guy."

She thought about arguing the point, particularly since she'd found an empty coffee cup stuffed under the counter where she kept the petri dishes. But Duane was the type who had to learn on his own.

"Have you finished the trial tests for the new lotion?"

"Finished number five today. It's good to go."

"We need six before we make that determination."

"I've had the same outcome for five. It's not going to change. Trust me."

"Did I tell you that I found a tattoo shop that does permanent eyebrows? Two hundred stabs of the needle and you won't have to worry about growing yours back.''

''Okay, okay. I'll do another test. What about you? Have you decided what we're going to do to spice up this stuff? How about a flavored lotion?''

''That's already been done.''

''We could do unusual flavors. Coffee. Peanut butter. Mmm.''

''We want to remind women of their sensuality, not what they had for lunch.''

''What about scented lotions?''

''That's already been done.''

''We could do unusual scents.''

''If you say coffee and peanut butter, I'm firing you.''

''Hey, everybody loves the smell of a good cup of coffee, and peanut butter's the universal bread spread.''

''Just finish the preliminary tests on the basic compound and feed the data into the computer. I'll plug in later and review everything.''

''So what's the zinger then?''

''I'm working on it.''

''I hope so. I'm getting claustrophobic in this tiny lab. I need some space. My own desk. My very own coffeemaker—''

''Did I hear slurping?''

''That was my stomach grumbling. All this talk has me hungry. And thirsty.''

''Keep it in the lunchroom.''

''Don't I always?''

Madeline hit the off button, dropped the phone into

her purse and glanced up in time to see Austin Jericho stroll out of Skeeter's. He crossed the street, his strides long and sure, and climbed into his pickup truck.

She still couldn't believe it. Austin Jericho had actually noticed her. And he'd remembered her. *And* he'd been attracted to her.

Madeline smiled. Maybe being home wouldn't be all that bad, after all.

SHE HAD TO FIND a hot man *now*.

A man was all that stood between Madeline and the fifty points she needed to prove to each of her old friends—as well as every other person at Cherry Blossom Junction—that she had, indeed, turned into the baddest babe in Texas.

Her focus shifted to the game card she'd just drawn.

> *If a bad girl is what you long to be,*
> *Forthright and daring are always key.*
> *Even the hottest man loves a bold miss,*
> *So prove yourself and give him a kiss!*

"What about him?" Every eye at the table turned to peer across the semicrowded dance floor.

"Girl, get out of here," Janice shook her head. "Your roots are showing, Eileen."

"What, like, is that supposed to mean?"

"That you've been married so long you've forgotten what *hot* means. We're not talking sweaty."

Eileen, a petite blonde, stiffened and straightened her baseball jersey that sported Team Mom in royal blue letters. "Well, when I, like, sweat, it usually means I'm hot."

"Ignore her," Janice told the other women. "She doesn't get out much. So what about him?" Janice wiggled her eyebrows and pointed out a man currently two-stepping around the dance floor, a smiling redhead in his arms. "He certainly can fill out a pair of Wrangler jeans."

"He's not very handsome." Brenda Chance, ex treasurer of the Chem Gems, adjusted her wire-framed, rose-tinted glasses.

Brenda worked as an interior designer in Austin now, but in her day she'd recited the elements table faster than anyone in Kendall County. While she had a practical head on her shoulders, she also had a romantic nature that had her wearing an old-fashioned lace dress that looked suspiciously like a pair of window sheers.

"That's definitely a face only his momma could love," Brenda went on. "My Cal has a great face." She sighed dreamily, then glanced around before zeroing in on another man. "What about him?" She smiled as she indicated the guy from their high school past voted Most Likely to Spit on Old People. "He's got nice eyes—the exact color of Cal's."

"Girl, he's about as nice as a pit bull," Janice said. "Besides, he's got puny arms. We need some muscle."

"And good hands," Sarah added.

Back in her day, Sarah Buchanan had been part of the in crowd, the only one among the Chem Gems. She'd been smart *and* beautiful *and* the baddest bad girl in Cadillac. She'd changed her ways the day of Sharon's death, however, and she now sat quietly, her long red hair pulled up in a tight ponytail, her mouth void of the red lipstick she'd always loved. Longing filled her eyes for a brief moment. "I used to love great hands on a guy."

"And a mustache," Brenda chimed in. "They're sooo dreamy. Cal has a mustache."

"They're lethal to supersensitive skin." The comment came from the bride-to-be. "She's supposed to kiss him, not break out."

"Let me get this straight." Brenda adjusted her glasses again. "She has to dance with him *and* kiss him?"

"If she wants to win the game," Sarah said.

"So what if she kisses him but doesn't dance with him? Does she get half the points?"

"Girl, it's all or nothing," Janice said.

"So does she, like, kiss first or, like, dance first?" Eileen asked.

"It doesn't matter." Madeline fingered the game card and scoped out prospects. "I could do either."

"You can't just walk up to a guy and kiss him," Brenda said. "It's too forward. Whatever would he think?"

Madeline smiled and indicated the game spread out on the table. "That maybe I'm the baddest babe in Texas?"

"I say you dance with him first," Cheryl Louise offered. "Talk a little. Then kiss him. It's more romantic." She sighed and gazed dreamily at a man standing near the bar. A group of men surrounded him, their beers lifted in salute. He glanced over his shoulder and smiled at her. She waved back. "That's how Jack and I met. He asked me to dance at the Charity Chili Chowdown last year. We ate and talked and swayed. Afterward he kissed me so softly and tenderly that I just knew he was the one."

"How totally sweet," Brenda sighed.

"How tame." Sarah looked wistful.

"How abnormal." Janice gave a shiver.

"I don't see how dancing and kissing and finding the man of your dreams can be construed as abnormal," Cheryl Louise said.

"The bride and the groom having their parties at the same small-time honky-tonk is what's whacked-out. Girl, how in God's green earth are you supposed to let your hair down with your fiancé a few feet away?"

"I don't have enough hair to let down. Besides, this is the only place in town that has a dance floor. The Pink Cadillac is much too small for two-stepping."

The Pink Cadillac was the only bar inside the city limits. It was a great place to get together to visit and suck down a few cold ones, but it didn't have the party atmosphere of a real sawdust-on-the-floor, country-crooning dance hall like Cherry Blossom Junction.

The bar was owned and operated by Eden Hallsey Weston, a bad girl in her own right who'd married the town's golden boy a few years ago. The news had shocked everyone, especially Madeline, who'd heard from Janice, who'd heard from Cheryl Louise, who'd been at the wedding. Eden had always been so outrageous while Brady had walked the straight and narrow path set forth by his conservative family. They'd been opposites, yet they'd fallen madly in love anyway. Just like in a fairy tale.

Madeline didn't do fairy tales. Hot, hunky, badass bad boys didn't gravitate toward shy, geeky good girls.

Which was why she'd traded in the old Madeline when she'd rolled out of Cadillac the day after Sharon's funeral. Maddie had seen for herself how precious life was, and she'd made up her mind then and there to live it to the fullest. That meant conquering her fears and taking chances. Being a bold, brazen woman who lived for the moment rather than the shy, geeky girl who'd spent her days dreaming and baking in her father's doughnut shop.

While she wished Eden and Brady the best of luck, she wanted more out of life than a husband and a handful of kids and a boring existence in a desperately small town.

Particularly since said town held so many bad memories. Of being a nerd and getting overlooked by the boy of her dreams, and losing her closest and dearest friend.

Her lungs constricted and she forced her attention back to her friends and the conversation.

"...could have driven to Austin," Janice pointed out. "I know this great little club that specializes in exotic male dancers."

"And get back at the crack of dawn? I need my beauty sleep for tomorrow."

"*Half-naked* exotic male dancers," Janice added.

"I like knowing that Jack is here." Cheryl Louise

waved again and Jack winked back before shifting his attention to his buddies.

"*Cute,* half-naked exotic male dancers."

"Give it up," Madeline told her. "G-strings don't interest a woman who's helplessly in love."

"Unless it's the man she loves wearing the G-string," Brenda pointed out. "Cal wears one for me."

"Come on, girls," Cheryl Louise said. "Madeline needs to find a guy and our yapping isn't going to help her concentrate."

"So who wants her to concentrate?" Sarah asked. "Sorry, Madeline, but I want to win."

"It's just a game," Cheryl Louise said, fingering the makeshift veil one of the girls had made for her. "A silly little game that's supposed to be fun."

"Girl, you say that because you're about to trade in your bad-girl status and promise not to be bad, but there are those of us who'd like to keep our reputation."

"You don't have a reputation," Cheryl Louise pointed out to Janice. "And you never had one. The only one who had anything remotely bad going for her was Sarah, and even she's as boring as they come now. No offense, Sarah," she said to the quiet redhead. "You're just anxious to win so you don't have to pick up Uncle Spur from the airport."

"Uncle Spur's coming to the wedding?" Madeline asked, her mind rushing back to her childhood and the ornery old man who'd come to visit Cheryl and Sharon every Christmas. He'd sat in the living room with his chewing tobacco and a soda can and offered an opinion on everything from making strawberry jam to the state of world politics. Uncle Spur had liked to talk. Even more, he'd liked being right.

"Of course he's coming," Cheryl Louise said. "He's my oldest living relative. I couldn't get married without Uncle Spur." As though she just noticed the effect of her news, her eyes narrowed. "What's wrong with Uncle Spur?"

"Nothing," Madeline said. "It's just…he's quite a character."

"An obnoxious character," Brenda added.

"He spit on me the last time I saw him," Janice said.

"He was just showing off," Cheryl Louise explained. "He was the Waller County Spit-Off champ back then. But then the cataracts set in and he came in third to his two brothers. He never spits now. Besides, I would pick him up myself, but I don't have time."

"Don't you worry about it," Madeline told her. "One of us will do it."

"Yep," Janice said. "The loser gets the privilege." She turned on Madeline. "Pick someone, or forfeit and let Sarah take her turn. She's next in line with points if you don't pull this off."

But Madeline wasn't forfeiting. It wasn't so much about winning—while Uncle Spur wasn't the most pleasant person, Madeline could endure a two-hour drive from the airport with him if it meant helping out a friend. Rather, this game was about conquering her fears and living life. About proving to all of her friends, and herself, that she truly had changed when she'd left the comfort of her small town for the excitement of the big city. About picking the hottest, hunkiest guy in the honky-tonk and approaching him as bold as you please.

Something the old Maddie would have been too frightened and embarrassed to do because she'd been more content to fantasize about life than actually live it.

No more.

She glanced around, found her target standing just inside the doorway and summoned her courage. Her moment of truth had finally arrived.

THIS WAS A BIG WASTE of time.

The truth echoed in Austin Jericho's brain the minute he stepped inside Cherry Blossom Junction, the one and only dance hall in Cadillac, Texas.

Not that Austin had anything against dance halls, particularly this one. The place had character. Once a train depot near the turn of the century, Cherry Blossom Junction was far from the typical Texas honky-tonk. Beers were served up from behind the original hand-carved ticket counters. Instead of a mechanical bull, the very first engine to chug out of the station sat in the far corner. Train schedules graced the walls rather than the typical neon beer signs. And when the band cranked up the "Orange Blossom Special," an authentic train whistle blew along with the music.

Nope, it sure-as-shootin' wasn't the place itself Austin had a problem with.

It's just that if a man had set his mind to add more fruit to his diet, he certainly wouldn't mosey over to the Dairy Freeze for a double-dipped. Likewise, if a gambler had decided to save his money rather than throw it away, he would damned sure stay far away from Pete, the numbers runner at the bingo hall.

Since Austin had decided to find himself a nice, quiet, conservative woman to settle down with him on his ranch, Cherry Blossom Junction was definitely at the bottom of his potential meet-market list. He needed to stick to church picnics and bake sales to find the kind of filly that would make him happy for the long haul, a goal he'd been working on for the past three weeks.

He'd narrowed it down to a handful of prospects— Debbie the kindergarten teacher, Christine the registered nurse at the retirement home, Angela the church choir director, Jennifer the head of the local Society for the Prevention of Cruelty to Animals and Claire who ran the town's only day care. They were all nice. Pretty. Wholesome. The trouble was, they all sort of blended together with their freshly baked apple pies and their show-me-the-ring-and-I'll-show-you-some-lovin' smiles, and he didn't have a clue which one to choose.

But he'd given his word to Miss Marshalyn Simmons and he aimed to keep it. Miss Marshalyn had been the town's librarian and expert cake baker for special events. She was also the most stubborn pig-headed woman ever to wag a finger at him and the closest thing to a mother he'd known since his own had passed away when he was five years old. He'd promised her that he would slow down and settle down in time for her going-away party—she was moving down to Florida to live with her sister. While the old woman wanted proof that he'd changed, she didn't expect him to find and marry someone before she left. She merely wanted to see him with a serious, suitable candidate. In return, she'd pledged one hundred acres of prime pastureland.

While he was more than willing to buy the land, she'd refused to sell it to him. She wanted peace of mind, not money, and so she'd made him an offer he couldn't refuse.

The land wasn't the only reason for his decision. While he'd reached a brick wall in his professional life—he needed that land to expand and beef up his herd—he'd also hit a big one in his personal life. A man could only work so much. When the sun set and the day was done, he had to head home.

But Austin didn't have a home. Sure, he had his own place, bought and paid for with his own sweat. But he didn't have a *home*—a warm, comforting place filled with plenty of laughter and good smells and warmth. Miss Marshalyn's house had had all three, and it had been the closest thing to a real home he'd known way back when.

He wanted his own now and a family to go with it, and that meant finding the right kind of woman. The kind who taught Sunday school and helped old ladies across the street. The kind who planted a vegetable garden and shelled peas and made candied sweet potatoes. The permanent kind who had more on her mind than one night.

All the more reason he should be anywhere but inside Cherry Blossom Junction.

"Hey, buddy. Over here!" The familiar voice drew Austin's attention.

His gaze shifted to the group of men clustered at the bar. Stetsons bobbed as heads turned and hands waved.

Austin couldn't help but grin at the group, particularly the cowboy wearing a foam ball and chain around his neck and a Kiss Me I'm The Groom button.

Jack Beckham was one of Austin's oldest friends and he was tying the knot tomorrow afternoon. Austin couldn't very well miss giving his buddy a grand send-off just because he was on a time limit to find himself a suitable wife.

"You're the last person I expected to see here. Shouldn't you be cruising the bingo hall right now?"

Austin turned to see his younger brother grinning back at him, a buxom blonde hanging on his arm.

"It's for a good cause. Besides, it's seniors' night and I'm looking for a woman a few years younger. I'm guessing you're not taking Miss Marshalyn up on her offer?"

Houston Jericho, Austin's middle brother and one of the best damned bull riders on the pro rodeo circuit, winked and pulled the blonde closer. "'Fraid not. I'm in no hurry to slow down and rope cows from now till kingdom come. That's your dream, bro."

"A man's got to grow up sometime."

Miss Marshalyn had made the same proposition to Houston when he'd surprised everybody and driven into town yesterday morning.

He'd been busy hitting every major rodeo in the United States, working his way up to the pro rodeo finals in Las Vegas in a few weeks. No one had expected him to take time off between rides to attend the wedding. But Houston and Jack went way back, as well. The man had been one of the few friends to all three Jericho brothers when they'd been kids.

And so Houston had come home.

But not to settle down, as he'd been quick to point out to Miss Marshalyn. Houston liked his life minus any roots. He was free, going where he wanted, when he wanted, and he intended to stay that way.

"I'll leave the growing old to you," he told his brother as he sipped a beer with his free hand.

"That's growing *up*."

"Same thing." Houston winked. "I've got more bulls to ride, and at least one woman I haven't had the pleasure of getting to know better." He winked at the woman on his arm. "Ain't that right, sugar?" He gave the blonde a quick kiss. "Besides, I like things just fine the way they are. Moving away from this place was the best thing I ever did."

"You mean running away, don't you?"

"I don't run from anyone or anything," he drawled, then turned and steered the blonde toward the dance floor. "Later, bro."

Austin stared after Houston. He was running, all right. From the past. From the legacy that had haunted all three of the Jericho brothers since birth. Dallas, the youngest, had made peace with his past last year when he'd married his childhood sweetheart. He and his wife were expecting their first child, and they were happy. Content.

Austin wanted the same.

That's what he told himself. But then he heard the soft, sexy, *familiar* voice. He felt a jolt of heat rush through him and suddenly he wanted something altogether different.

"Excuse me."

He felt a tap on his shoulder and turned to find himself staring into a pair of bright green eyes. The same eyes that had stared at him over an extralarge box of lubricated condoms earlier that day.

For the first time since Austin had vowed to find a wife, he actually wondered if maybe, just maybe, he wasn't making a big mistake. Because suddenly hot and heavy sex in the here and now seemed a heck of a lot more appealing than peace and contentment somewhere in the far-off future.

# 3

_EASY, HOSS._

Austin took a deep breath and tried to steady himself as one all-important fact registered—this was Maddie Hale. The bookworm who'd spent class time listening rather than writing notes back and forth with her friends.

Actually she'd written one note, but he'd done his damnedest in the past twelve years to forget all about the poetic declaration of love he'd happened upon purely by accident. He'd also tried to forget those few tension-filled moments standing near the concession stand when he'd looked at her, really _looked_ at her, for the very first time.

Love note aside, she was still the shy girl who'd blushed at him from the safety of an algebra book and brought him homemade muffins.

The innocent who'd never once ventured behind the bleachers during a football game.

He knew the backside of those bleachers by heart. Hell, he'd carved most of those names himself and hers was not among the bunch. He'd be willing to bet his finest horse that she didn't even know about the conquest bench. What's more, he would lay down his entire spread that she'd never set her fine little bottom down and kissed up a Gulf hurricane with one of the locals, either.

Maddie had been too nice and wholesome and respectable for bleacher smooching. And that afternoon at Skeeter's he'd been wrong to think she was anything but the same sweet girl now.

The proof dangled from Cheryl Louise's head.

He stared past the top of Maddie's soft blond hair, that smelled of sweet strawberries and cream, to the group of women sitting nearby.

A drape of white tulle decorated with condom packages sat atop the bride-to-be's head. Six to be exact. The same brand, same size Maddie had purchased that afternoon. Obviously they hadn't been meant for her personal use.

A crazy assumption in the first place. Maddie wasn't the condom type. She was the quiet, mild, I'm-saving-it-all-for-the-man-of-my-dreams kind of girl. Why, she made muffins, for Chrissake! Big, giant, melt-in-your-mouth homemade blueberry muffins. Sure, they couldn't compete with a bowl of Miss Marshalyn's candied sweet potatoes, but they came in a close second.

Now that Austin had given up fast times and even faster women, Maddie was exactly his type of woman. On top of that, she was an old friend. The only female, in fact, who'd ever qualified for such a title.

Austin Jericho had never kept company with girls he'd had no sexual interest in. He'd always wanted something from them and they'd wanted something from him—namely a good round of red-hot, breath-stealing sex. Or several rounds.

Not Maddie.

The only thing she'd wanted from him had been his daily homework assignment and his full attention when she was explaining the newest algebra equation.

There'd been no sly glances, no fluttering eyelashes or wandering hands or heaving cleavage. Hell, he'd never even known she had cleavage, thanks to the sacklike flower-print dresses she'd always worn.

Except for that Friday night at the football game. She'd worn a red sweater and blue jeans and he'd actually realized she had a figure. Nice, round hips. Large breasts. But while shapely, the clothes hadn't been revealing.

Not like what she wore now.

His attention shifted back to her and the enticing display of creamy flesh fully visible above the neckline of her black leather tank top. His gut hollowed for a long moment and his mouth went dry.

*Easy,* he told himself.

So what if she had visible cleavage? That didn't mean she'd checked her morals at the door and turned into a bona fide, red-hot, give-it-to-me-now wild woman.

This was Maddie, he reminded himself, drawing a long pull on his beer.

The only girl he'd actually been able to talk to about stuff, like his love of horses and his desperation to do something other than perpetuate his family's no-good reputation. He hadn't worried about impressing her or sweeping her off her feet. He'd never even thought about her like *that.*

Okay, maybe that once, when he'd opened her love letter. But when he'd asked her about it at the football game, she'd sworn that it hadn't been meant for him. He'd let things go at that, and he'd let her go. He'd walked off with Barbara Mayfield for a wild ride on his Harley and an even wilder ride in the back of her daddy's old pickup.

His attention snagged on her lips. Soft, full, kissable lips. His heart bucked and his blood rushed and a certain part of his anatomy, a certain *hard* part, throbbed just thinking about what she would taste like.

"What do you say?" she asked, her sweet voice pushing past the pounding of his heart. "Are you up for a little two-stepping?"

He was up, all right. But his throbbing erection had little to do with dancing and everything to do with Maddie.

*It's Madeline. No one really calls me Maddie anymore.*

He could see why. She looked too sophisticated, too sexy, too...*hot.*

So?

Even if the package looked a little different, this was still Maddie. *Nice, wholesome, respectable Maddie.*

He smiled, set his beer on the bar and reached for her hand. "Lead the way, darlin'."

THERE WAS NOTHING NICE, wholesome or respectable about the sexy woman in his arms.

The thought struck him the moment they moved onto the dance floor and she stepped into his arms.

The two-step had faded into a slow, sweet, cryin' tune that required a little more contact than he'd anticipated. Her arms slid around his neck. Her full breasts pressed against his chest. Her pelvis cradled his, moving against him with a soft, subtle sway that sent a bolt of electricity straight from his hard-on to his brain.

The jolt scrambled his sanity, and instead of pushing her away and running for safety, he pulled her even closer and closed his eyes.

Her hair tickled the underside of his jaw. Her strawberries-and-cream scent filled his head. Her luscious curves pressed against his hard body. Her warmth seeped inside and made his blood rush faster.

His hand slid an inch lower, easing from the small of her back to the swell of her sweet little ass molded by the tight miniskirt. His other hand slid up her back, under the spill of hair to cup the back of her neck. His fingers pressed into her flesh and his thumb drew lazy circles against the tender spot just below her ear. If he hadn't known better, he would have sworn he heard her sigh—a soft, breathy sound that meant she liked his touch.

That it turned her on. That she wanted more. Right here. Right now.

For a split second, he inched toward her nipple puckered beneath the slick material of her halter top. He wanted desperately to slide his fingers beneath the plunging neckline and tease the ripe tip…

*Slow down.*

She was not the sort of girl to get busy on the dance floor in front of half the damned town. She was a good girl. Tame rather than wild. He had to slow down and behave himself.

His eyes popped open. He eased his hold and drew back to a respectable distance.

"What's wrong?" She stared up at him, her green eyes glittering beneath the swirl of colored dance-hall lights. Her forehead wrinkled and he had the sudden urge to reach up and smooth the lines away with his fingertip. "Austin?" Surprise turned to concern. "Are you okay?"

"Um, yeah. I just think we need to slow things down a little."

Instead of smiling because he was being a proper gentleman, she frowned. "I think things were going just fine."

"We were moving too fast. Way too fast. I don't like fast."

"Since when?" She eyed him. "You were always racing around on your motorcycle, burning rubber down Main Street, and burning up the sheets with some lucky girl afterward."

"How do you know I burned up the sheets?"

She stared up at him, a knowing look in her wide green eyes. Not a plain old grass green at all, but a deep, vibrant shade of jade that glittered and teased and dared him when she smiled.

Like now.

"Word gets around. You definitely liked fast."

"The only thing fast in my life now is my cutting horse. Speaking of which—" he checked his watch "—I have to be up early and it's getting late." He pinned her with a stare. "Way past your bedtime if memory serves me." She'd always been bright eyed in the morning. Always well rested from a full night's sleep while he'd been barely able to keep his eyes open in class.

"That was before I realized what I was missing." She gestured toward the table of women, their drinks raised in a toast. She waved. "The party's just getting started."

"I never figured you for a party girl."

"Oh, I love parties!"

"Since when?"

"Since I left this hole-in-the-wall town and realized what I was missing."

"A vicious hangover the morning after?"

"Hours of fun the night before." Her eyes sparkled with meaning and his body throbbed. "Don't be such a fuddy-duddy. At least finish the dance before you call it a night." She stepped up against him and twined her arms around his neck again.

He drew a deep breath and resisted the urge to pull her close and show her what she could do with her *fuddy-duddy*. Instead, he anchored his hands on her waist and did his damnedest to ignore the heat seeping into his fingertips and the sweet scent teasing his nostrils.

"So how are the libraries in Dallas?" he blurted,

eager to prove that she was still the girl he remembered.

She'd loved the library. She'd spent every afternoon sitting in the corner with her nose buried in a book, a muffin beside her, while life at Cadillac High had passed her by. "Huge, I bet. Fully stocked with everything from *Madame Bovary* to *The Life and Times of Marie Curie*." He recited two of the books he'd seen her with way back when.

"Actually, I've never been to a library in Dallas. I'm too busy."

"You probably spend all your time in your lab. You were always holed up in the chemistry room when you weren't in the library."

"I do spend a lot of time at work, but not just in the lab. I've got marketing meetings and product demonstrations, and I do try to take time off to have fun."

He remembered the so-called social activities she and her geeky friends had engaged in on Friday and Saturday nights when everyone else had been at football games or out cruising in their cars. Only sexy Sarah who'd had a reputation almost as bad as Austin's had been the exception. "Poetry readings and baking?"

"Bungee jumping and rock concerts."

His eyebrows shot up. "Rock concerts?"

"Creed. I've seen them twice. My first time, I marked the occasion with this." She moved the veil of blond hair hanging over one shoulder and turned so he could see the back of one delectable shoulder. A small red devil smiled back at him.

A she-devil. As in hot, as in wild, as in *give it to me now*.

While his mind tried to register the fact that sweet, demure Maddie Hale had a tattoo, his body simply reacted. His mouth went dry. His heart jumped. The hard-on stretching his jeans tight throbbed in anticipation.

"It was my first concert and I went a little crazy."

He swallowed and searched for his voice. "Damn straight you did," he finally croaked.

"I was going to get something a little more tame, like a heart or Tweety Bird or something *cute*. But then I saw this and thought, what the hell? I can be as wild as the next woman."

Hardly. She was sweet. Wholesome. Respectable. She *couldn't* have changed that much, and Austin intended to prove it.

"You still eat blueberry muffins every afternoon?" He zeroed in on the memory of her sitting in the library, munching away as she waited for him. "One jumbo muffin every day at four."

"Sure do."

He drew in a deep breath. *See? She hasn't changed that much.*

"English muffins. No butter." At his outraged look, she added, "A girl's got to watch her figure."

Okay, so she'd climbed the thermometer a few degrees since high school. She was counting calories, worrying about keeping her curvaceous body in shape so that she could show it off with revealing clothes rather than flower-print dresses.

So what?

A great figure and revealing clothes and a party life *and* a tattoo didn't mean she truly had morphed into the exact type of woman he'd sworn off when he'd made up his mind to settle down.

"But you loved blueberry muffins, and people shouldn't give up things they love because society tells them to." He recited the words she'd told him every time she'd seen one of the "in" girls scarfing carrot sticks. She'd wrinkled her nose and given him a lecture about society's oppression of women, and how he should open his mind to all sorts of beauty. And he'd enjoyed every minute. Very few people had ever cared enough about his opinion to try to change it.

Except Maddie.

"Muffins are way too fattening."

"You always wore a bike helmet when you pedaled around town on that three-speed of yours." He was grasping, but a guy had to do what a guy had to do.

"Yeah, but now I like to feel the breeze blow through my hair. I even graduated to a ten-speed." Her eyes lit. "It's really fast."

"You always carried an umbrella even when there wasn't a cloud in the sky."

She shrugged. "It's fun getting caught in the rain."

"The girl I remember wouldn't be caught dead wearing a leather halter top in a place like this."

"And the boy I remember wouldn't be wasting time talking with a woman wearing a leather halter top in a place like this when he could be doing other, more important, things."

"What's that supposed to mean?"

She eyed him, licked her lips and murmured, "Kiss me."

Austin stared at her damp mouth for one heart-stopping moment and imagined what she would taste like.

Tart, like the wine she'd been drinking. And hot. Like the woman she'd become—his hottest, most erotic fantasy.

"Pretty please."

Her soft plea pushed past the frantic pounding of his heart and chipped away at his resolve.

He drank in a deep breath of her, let his gaze linger on her slick, full lips for a long, hungry moment and then Austin did the only thing a man who'd made up his mind to settle down for good could do—he turned and walked the other way.

Because Austin had given up indulging his fantasies. A fantasy was temporary. One night. Maybe a few if it was a really good fantasy. But he wanted more. He wanted each day, every day, from here on out. He wanted to plant roots and build a home and make babies with a woman who wanted the same.

The new and improved Madeline Hale, with her big-city ways and her big-city life, had one-night stand written all over her.

# 4

---

"HERE'S THE FLIGHT NUMBER and the arrival time." Cheryl Louise scribbled the information on a napkin the next morning as she sat across from Madeline at Chester's Diner.

Madeline slathered fat-free yogurt on her whole-wheat toast and did her best to ignore the smell drifting from across the table of pancakes drenched in butter and syrup. While she indulged in Oreos for the sake of creativity, there was nothing at stake now except her deprived taste buds.

Back in Dallas, it was so much easier to keep her normal routine. She worked so hard that she barely had time to think about food. When she did, it was much easier to shake the cravings. She had only to glance around V.A.M.P.'s executive offices at the svelte women in their designer suits and name-brand shoes to motivate herself. Maddie had spent her entire adolescence not fitting in. No more. She fit in just fine back in Dallas.

Here in Cadillac, there wasn't a Gucci jacket or a pair of leather Pradas in sight. There was food. Lots of home-cooked, mouthwatering food. And conversation. And...warmth.

She shook the thought away and fixed her attention on the nervous bride-to-be sitting across the scarred Formica tabletop.

"Make sure you're there early and make sure you've got a sign or something so he'll know who you are."

"He's on a commuter flight with eighty pounds of horse feed and three new hogs for the Double D Ranch. The only other person who'll be at the airport is old Mr. Denton. I doubt I could get lost in the crowd."

"Promise you'll carry a sign. His eyesight isn't what it used to be. And Uncle Spur's not used to being in the big city."

"We're in Cadillac. Population three thousand. No McDonald's. No after-hours grocery store. No tanning bed."

"Donna Mae Walters over at the Toss-n-Tease put in a stand-up tanning unit last year."

"Okay, so the town's come of age. It still doesn't qualify as a huge metropolis." At Cheryl's worried expression, she added, "I'll keep the radio on an AM farm station and we won't go near the Toss-n-Tease. That way he won't have major culture shock."

"Thanks so much." Cheryl Louise smiled and nibbled at her pancakes. "I was hoping you'd be the one to do this. The other girls tend to let him get under their skin. The last time he came down for my graduation, he told Sarah that she should stop coloring her hair and let it go natural."

"Red *is* her natural color."

"That's what she told Uncle Spur, but then he demanded proof."

"But how could she prove…" Her thoughts trailed off as she did a mental evaluation of all the possibilities. Realization dawned and her eyes widened. "He didn't."

"He didn't mean it in a sexual way, of course. He's a sweet old man, but practical. He handed her a pair of tweezers."

"Ouch." She grinned. "I bet Sarah told him where to get off."

"Believe it or not, she went through with it and proved him wrong. Not that it was enough. He said it wasn't hers and he wouldn't settle for anything less than a DNA match to verify ownership." Her voice lowered. "He's sort of bored out there and I think he watches a little too much TV at times. Anyway, she said no, but then he came after her with a pair of scissors. He didn't catch her, of course, but by the end of the party, she was in tears."

"Tears? Our Sarah? She's never cried over anyone or anything." Except once, at Sharon's funeral. They'd all cried, except for Madeline. It had taken all of her strength just to stand beside the grave and breathe. Afterward she'd climbed into her car and left her small unsophisticated, going-nowhere town far behind, the way Sharon had always wanted to.

Sharon?

No, Maddie had wanted to leave, as well, and she'd done just that. She'd left her old life, her old self and her haunting memories of that night, and headed off to pursue her own dreams.

*And boy, have I got a piece of beachfront property smack-dab in the middle of Kansas to sell you.*

She ignored the nagging voice and the image that niggled at the back of her mind. A clear, star-studded sky. A gravel road. An enormous tree…

She shifted in her seat, suddenly anxious to *do* something. "Can I have a bite?" she blurted before reaching over for a piece of Cheryl's pancakes.

The sugary sweet flavor of maple exploded on her tongue and consumed her senses, and she concentrated on chewing.

"Um, sure. In fact, I'm not really hungry." She slid the plate toward Madeline. "Anyhow, he scared off Sarah right then and there. The others are just as leery of him, but I know you won't let Uncle Spur ruffle you."

Way back when maybe.

But not now. She dealt with snotty marketing personnel and a bitch of a research director on a daily basis. She could hold her own with a difficult old man.

"I can handle it," she said, taking another bite. She would have to handle it, because she'd lost the game.

Thanks to Austin.

One measly kiss. That's all she'd wanted from him. She might as well have asked for his balls on a platter. That's how horrified he'd looked when she'd made the request.

Far from the reaction she'd anticipated, considering that he'd actually given her The Look with those liquid blue eyes. The Look that said I want you and I aim to have you.

Not that she'd ever been on the receiving end of one of his legendary looks. He'd reserved those for the school bad girls who'd always flocked around him. But for a little while last night, she'd felt like one of those bold women instead of the shy, frumpy goody-goody she'd been all those years ago. She'd felt truly attractive and drop-dead gorgeous and *wanted*.

Felt? To hell with that. She *was* all three, even if Austin Jericho hadn't recognized it. He was obviously still stuck in the past, viewing her in all her Gem glory.

Geeky.

Brainy.

Matronly.

As the familiar words she'd heard from her peers time and time again echoed through her head, she became aware of the mouthful of syrup and pancakes tantalizing her taste buds. She swallowed and pushed the plate away.

Cheryl glanced at her watch. "I have to run. I'll meet you at the house later to introduce you to my plants and go over Twinkles's hygiene schedule."

Twinkles had a hygiene schedule?

The question echoed through her mind and another sliver of apprehension went through her. Madeline fought it back down and smiled. Twinkles was just a dog, even if he did have a hygiene schedule, and Madeline liked dogs. While she didn't actually have an animal of her own—she wasn't home enough to take care of one—she'd always loved cute, cuddly puppies. As for the plants...how hard could daily watering be?

"Have fun at the hairdresser and try to enjoy the rest of the day."

"I'll enjoy the honeymoon, especially knowing that you're looking out for Twinkles and my girls." She stood and gathered up her purse and bridal book. "Oh, and don't forget the sign. Uncle Spur can't see to save his life."

"WELL, WELL. Just call me a three-legged jackrabbit and put me out of my misery if it ain't Maddie Hale."

Time seemed to have stood still for Spur Tucker. He'd looked ancient then with his shock of snow-white hair and his leathery skin, and he'd changed little. He stooped a fraction more and his hair had thinned some. Otherwise, he was every bit the man she remembered from all those childhood Christmases, with the exception of his eyes. Rather than cloudy and gray as they'd been back then, they were now a clear, crystal blue.

She peered closer. "You know who I am?" She hadn't even held up her sign, complete with extra bold letters.

"'Course I do. What do you think I am, blind or something?"

"Well," she started, but he cut her off.

"Well, I ain't. Cataract surgery. My vision's as first-rate as the rest of me."

"That's good."

"'Course it is." His face crinkled as he narrowed

his eyes and sized her up. "I see you still got plenty of meat on them bones of yours."

"And I see you're still every bit as charming."

"'Course I am, and I'm also a whole lot wiser." He handed several bags to her and picked up the lightest. "Speaking of which, let's get going 'cause I ain't of a mind to waste time. I got things to do."

"The wedding's not until later tonight." Madeline picked up the largest bag and her shoulder wrenched. "You've got time for a little nap."

"A *nap?* Hells bells, I ain't got time to sleep. I still have to shower and shave, polish my boots, squirt on some of the vanilla extract I packed just for special occasions. I aim to look and smell my Sunday best."

"I'm sure Cheryl Louise will appreciate that." She hoisted bag number two. "You must have packed an awful big bottle of vanilla."

"Those are extra vittles. A man's got to eat and I know how you women are. Why, you're liable to torture me with rabbit food for the next few days." He gave her another once-over. "'Course you probably got some vittles of your own stashed away. Why, you could probably hibernate a good six months with what you got stored in them hips of yours."

She let the suitcase slip from her hands and watched his look go from smug to panicked as his luggage dropped to the floor.

"Whoops, sorry about that," she muttered.

"Lordy be, just tote the danged thing. Don't throw it around." He shook his head. "And all the primping ain't for Cheryl Louise. It's for the future Mrs. Spur Nathaniel Elijah James Tucker.''

"You're engaged?"

"Sure am." He cleared his throat. "Well, I will be once I narrow down the playing field. I figure that ought to take a good fifteen minutes. Maybe ten. There are a lot of prime cutting horses at the Newfolk Auction, too, but I can always pick the best of 'em in less than ten minutes."

"You really intend to find a wife this weekend?" She struggled after him with the bags.

"That's why I'm here."

"I thought you were here for Cheryl Louise's wedding."

"It's called killing two hogs with one load of buckshot. Since this here's a social event, I thought I'd do double duty. Pay my respects to the bride and groom and find my own little bride to fetch back home." He picked up his steps. "Enough of this chitchat. Get a move on. I don't aim to keep the future missus waitin'."

SHE SHOULD HAVE BOUGHT the bread maker.

Madeline came to that conclusion the minute she walked inside Cheryl Louise's family home two hours later and came face-to-face with Twinkles.

Literally.

Twinkles was a Great Dane and far, far removed from the cute and cuddly puppy stage. Standing on his hind legs, his paws braced on her shoulders, he looked her straight in the eye. His snout bopped her in the nose. A fat, wet tongue flopped out and licked at her face.

"He's really...big," she told Sarah, who'd met her at the house since Cheryl Louise was still stuck at the hairdresser.

"He's big and several years old, but still as playful as a puppy."

"Is that where he got the name Twinkles?"

"'Twinkle, Twinkle Little Star' is his favorite lullaby. He likes to hear it every night after his evening walk." Sarah grabbed a spiral notebook from the nearby coffee table and flipped several pages. "He likes 'Mary Had A Little Lamb' after his morning walk, which should follow *Live with Regis and Kelly*—that's his favorite TV show." She held up the notebook. "It's all right here. There's a detailed schedule for feeding and hygiene, as well as a page with lyrics in case you're not up on your lullabies. And a TV schedule, as well. Oh, Cheryl also included a picture diagram of Twinkles with a list of the exact spots where he likes to be scratched. The last few pages contain information on the plants. They're all on the sun porch out back. Each pot is labeled with a name and an age."

"And a lullaby?"

"Actually, they like country music. There's a CD player out back complete with a stack of George Strait CDs. Each is labeled with a time slot and a preferred song." Sarah must have noticed Madeline's shocked look. "Look on the bright side, at least Tilly the farting poodle is going with them. Besides, it's only two weeks. They almost went to Australia, which would have meant a solid three.''

"Want to time-share with me?"

"I went for a popcorn maker myself. Speaking of which, I need to get going. I have to run by my house and grab the gift before I head for the church. I picked up the dresses at the dry cleaners. Yours is hanging over there.''

Madeline managed to dodge another lick and twist away from Twinkles. She crossed the living room and took a closer look at the dress hanging from the window casing.

"It's really orange."

"Cheryl Louise calls it coral."

"And frilly."

"She wanted a traditional Southern-belle look."

Twinkles walked up behind Madeline and started sniffing her backside. "I must be deranged."

"Why didn't you just get something off her bridal registry?"

"I thought house-sitting would be more personal."

"You're right about that." Sarah laughed as Twinkles stood on his hind legs and went for another wet lick. The sound died the minute she heard the door creak open. She turned to see Uncle Spur hobble over the threshold.

Madeline had left him to finish one of his atrocious cigars on the porch. A cloud of smoke and smell surrounded him.

"You remember Uncle—achewww!" Madeline sneezed once, twice, while doing her best to avoid

Twinkles and her overzealous affection. She'd never been allergic to dog hair, but then she'd never had a dog right in her face either.

"Say it, don't spray it," Uncle Spur grumbled as he walked past Madeline and headed for the stairs. "I'm in the second room to the left. Hurry up and get the bags out of the car. I need plenty of grooming time before I go hunting. Hey there, Red," he said to Sarah, who turned a noticeable shade of white and backed up a few steps. "Or so you say."

"I, um, really need to go," Sarah mumbled as she snatched up her purse, careful to keep her eye on Uncle Spur as she backed her way around him. "See you at the church."

"Where's the dye queen running off to in such a hurry?" Uncle Spur stared at the open doorway and watched Sarah hightail it out to her car.

"She's a natural redhead."

"And you're a size three."

She glared at the old man. "Are you always so pleasant?"

He frowned. "Damn straight I am, and don't you forget it." He turned and hobbled up the stairs. "Get moving. I got things to do."

"Sic 'em, boy," Madeline whispered as Uncle Spur disappeared up the stairs. The dog just wagged his tail and came at Madeline for another sloppy kiss. "Just my luck," she grumbled, twisting her head to the side to dodge the massive tongue. "I get stuck with a lover when what I really need is a fighter."

"I REALLY HAVE TO get up early tomorrow morning," Austin said as he tugged at the collar of his starched western shirt. "Can't we just skip the reception and call it quits for tonight?"

"And be rude? Nonsense." Marshalyn Simmons patted Austin's arm as they stood at the entrance to the Veterans of Foreign Wars Hall. "Besides, this place is full of nice, respectable women."

And a few not so nice and respectable women.

Austin zeroed in on Madeline Hale where she stood in the buffet line. Her voice echoed in his head.

*Kiss me.*

He'd wanted to do just that, and more. But he'd made a promise, to himself as well as Miss Marshalyn. It was high time he settled down, and with a woman *unlike* Madeline Hale. While she'd qualified as a good girl way back when, she'd obviously changed. He didn't intend to waste any of the precious time he had left—two weeks to be exact—on a one-night stand.

He knew that, yet with her standing right in his line of vision, looking so sweet and delicious in a dress that made him think of a nice, juicy, sugar-coated orange slice candy, he wasn't so sure. He'd always had a sweet tooth for orange slices. How many times had he scraped his pennies and nickels together to head down to Skeeter's and buy himself a bag?

Afterward, he would sit on the schoolhouse playground and indulge until he'd finished the last one. He'd gotten sick a time or two, but the few minutes of heaven while he'd savored the sweet treat had been worth a stomachache.

Just like all his wild nights spent drinking and carousing and burning up the sheets had been worth an awkward morning after, or so he'd thought.

Until he'd served as best man for Dallas's wedding last year. As Austin had watched his wild and reckless sibling recite his wedding vows, he'd started to think that maybe, just maybe, there was something to this commitment business. Particularly since his youngest brother had looked so *happy*.

His focus shifted in time to see Dallas help his very pregnant wife into a chair and give her a kiss before heading off to fetch her some punch. He wore his usual I've-got-a-good-woman grin, and Austin couldn't help but want a grin like that of his own.

Dallas's wife, Laney, would make a hell of a mother. One who would bake cookies and sing lullabies and do all of the things Sissy Jericho had never done for her three boys.

Then again, Sissy had been a mother by default rather than choice. She'd gotten pregnant at sixteen and, because her parents had been religious zealots, they'd forced her into marriage with the baby's father. Bick Jericho hadn't been any more ready or willing to be a parent than Sissy, but he'd had no choice. Either get married and do the right thing, or go to jail since he was eighteen and considered an adult. He'd chosen marriage.

But for a man as wild as the bulls he'd ridden on the rodeo circuit, marriage had turned out to be a prison in itself. He'd been unhappy and his wife had been unhappy, and neither had been able to curb their wild streaks. They'd partied too much, drunk too much, and fought too much.

When Austin's mother passed away from kidney failure—due to her diabetes and complications with the birth of her last child—his father had continued to party and drink and fight with any and everyone in his path. Right up until he'd dropped dead from a heart attack, thanks to liver problems.

Austin was breaking the cycle. He wasn't his father, even if he had been following the same path for the biggest part of his life. He was making something of himself, professionally and personally. Which was exactly why he intended to stay on this side of the room. With a full fifty feet of dance floor and tables between them, Maddie Hale wouldn't be much of a temptation.

With that thought in mind, Austin steered Miss Marshalyn straight to the groom's cake table.

"Why, there's Debbie Bernard," Miss Marshalyn told him. "She's the kindergarten teacher."

"We've already met. She's nice." He reached for a piece of groom's cake. There was just something about dancing with Debbie in full view of God and everybody, especially Maddie Hale, that didn't sit too well.

"She's more than nice. She makes an excellent pot roast. Why don't you ask her to dance?"

"She looks busy."

"Not really—oh, there's Christine Jackson. She's that LVN over at the Cadillac Nursing Home."

"I know. I've met her, too. She's real nice."

"She's more than nice. She's just itching to settle

down. Mabel Jasper is her next-door neighbor and she says that the girl's got a hope chest filled with china and she subscribes to *Brides* magazine. That's a dead giveaway. Why don't you ask *her* to dance?''

"She looks tired." He indicated her shoes, which she'd slid off before propping her feet on a nearby chair.

"Nonsense—hey, how about Angela Connally?'' She motioned toward a petite redhead loading her plate at a nearby buffet. "She sings like an angel and she volunteers down at the shelter twice a week. She has such a good heart.''

"I know. She's nice, too.''

"And desperate,'' Miss Marshalyn informed him. "She's been a bridesmaid fourteen times in the past five years. No girl wants to spend her life being a bridesmaid and never a bride. Why, I bet she's itching to find a nice man of her own. Why don't you ask *her* to dance?''

"She looks hungry." He indicated the plateful of little smoky sausages she held in her hands. The woman reached for a barbecue spare rib and Austin let loose a low whistle. "*Real* hungry. Speaking of which,'' he turned to the groom's cake table and reached for a shiny silver fork, "I've been waiting all week for this." He hadn't had the pleasure of sinking his teeth into one of Miss Marshalyn's desserts since Dallas and Laney's wedding last year.

The old woman smiled at his eagerness. "It has been a long time, hasn't it?''

"Too long." He shoved in a forkful of cake and

did his best not to spew it back out as the taste hit him.

"You always did like my fudge decadence, didn't you?"

He managed a nod and blinked to keep the tears from running out of his eyes.

"Is it as good as you remember?"

"Good doesn't even begin to describe this," he finally murmured when he'd managed to swallow.

She beamed. "I was a little worried. It smelled a little different while it was baking. Sort of tart. I thought maybe the grocer had mislabeled some of my spices."

Or maybe she'd misread some of them. In the past six months, Miss Marshalyn had been losing her eyesight to cataracts. A condition she refused to acknowledge, much less correct.

Austin had done his best to convince her to have the recommended surgery, but she'd been adamant that nothing was wrong. Having lost her husband of fifty-two years during routine gall-bladder surgery, she refused to have anything to do with doctors and hospitals and the proposed surgery, no matter how minor.

He couldn't blame her and so he did his best to help out whenever she asked.

"Oh, my Lord if it isn't Spur Tucker." Miss Marshalyn's voice drew Austin.

He turned to see the old man, hat in his hands, his few sparse hairs slicked to the side. "Cheryl Louise's uncle?"

"And the most obnoxious man in Texas. He's simply awful. Why, the last time he came for a visit, he actually spit a wad of tobacco on the tip of Lorissa Alcott's shoe.'' She squinted her eyes. ''Character aside, he does seem to have aged very well. Looks as vigorous as ever.''

If Austin had doubted her waning sight on occasion, he had proof now. Spur Tucker looked many things— anxious, grouchy and unpleasant—but vigorous wasn't one of them.

''Well, eat up,'' she said, turning back to the table. She motioned to the monstrous chocolate cake covered with a mountain of sugar-dusted raspberries. It stood virtually untouched while a line had formed at the bride's cake table a few feet away, which held the white confection Betty Eugene Norman had supplied. ''There's plenty more where that came from.''

''Excuse me, would you like to dance?'' The soft female voice caressed his ears, giving him a prime excuse to abandon the rest of his cake.

''Why, I sure would—'' The words stalled when he turned to find himself staring into Maddie's greener-than-green eyes.

''Why, it's little Maddie Hale,'' Miss Marshalyn exclaimed. ''How nice!''

''Madeline,'' she corrected. ''And it's nice to see you, too, Miss Marshalyn.'' She smiled at Austin. ''I think they're playing our song.''

The same slow, sweet waltz that had poured from the speakers at Cherry Blossom Junction filled the small hall, and a surge of heat went through him.

''Go on.'' Miss Marshalyn nudged him. ''You

shouldn't keep a lady waiting. Particularly the lady who helped you ace your algebra final. Besides, I see your younger brother is in sore need of some guidance right now.''

Before Austin could protest, she made a beeline for Houston, who stood in the far corner talking to a very tall brunette wearing a very skimpy dress.

''Why, that Missy Donovan gets around more than Bud the mailman,'' Miss Marshalyn's voice carried over her shoulder. ''She's the last sort of woman that boy should be wasting his time with....''

''She gives good advice,'' Maddie said, once Miss Marshalyn was out of earshot. ''If I were you, I'd take it. Come on and dance.''

He eyed her up and down. ''You're not a lady anymore.''

''Really?'' Damned if she didn't look excited at the prospect.

His gaze narrowed. ''A lady doesn't ask a man to kiss her after just one dance.''

''It wasn't one dance. It was half a dance, and I didn't ask you to kiss me. I *told* you to kiss me.''

''What is it with you?''

''What do you mean?''

He shook his head, plopped his cake plate on the table and ushered her off to a far corner of the room. He hauled her behind a large potted palm draped in white tulle and turned on her. ''You're a completely different person.''

Her face brightened. ''You really think so?''

''You used to be so...nice.''

"Nice girls finish last."

"At least they finish." His jaw clenched. "Do you know how dangerous it is to go around kissing strange men?"

"You're not strange." Her eyes danced. "Then again, maybe you are. There aren't too many normal, red-blooded men who would turn down a kiss with a willing woman."

"Is that so?"

"Which tells me that maybe you've shifted your focus from totally hot women to totally hot—"

"I like women," he cut in. "I like them just fine."

"Then what's the problem?"

"The problem is, I've got priorities, and kissing isn't one of them. I intend to settle down."

"With who?"

"I haven't decided yet."

She stared at him as if he'd grown an extra eye in the middle of his forehead. "It must be something in the water."

"What do you mean?"

"Uncle Spur's set on settling down, too, and intent on finding himself a wife in the next two days."

"For a man to think he can find a wife in two days is crazy."

"Finally the voice of reason."

"He needs at least two weeks, which is how long I've got until Miss Marshalyn's going-away party."

She gave him a look of bewilderment and disbelief and then shook her head resignedly. "So how about a dance in the meantime?"

"I don't think that would be such a good idea."

She arched an eyebrow at him. "Afraid you won't be able to control yourself?"

"If memory serves me, *you* wanted to kiss *me* during that dance. Hell, the dancing was probably just a front to move in for the kill."

"Actually, the dancing was for real. It was part of Who's the Baddest Babe?—this game we played last night at the bachelorette party. I had to pick a hot man, dance with him and kiss him in order to get fifty points. I lost because of you."

And the game's over now, Madeline told herself. She'd lost to Sarah and paid the price by picking up Uncle Spur. She had nothing more to gain by pursuing Austin Jericho.

Except the kiss that should have been hers over twelve years ago when they'd stood near the concession stand. Before she'd chickened out, denied the love note she'd written to him and watched him walk away with Big Boobs Barbara.

"If you lost, then why did you ask me to dance just now?" His eyes gleamed with challenge and something else. Something dark and delicious and forbidden to good girls the world over.

"Because I don't lose. I never lose. Forty-eight chemistry competitions, and I won every one. Last night was a gross injustice and—"

His mouth caught the rest of her words as he pressed his lips to hers. Suddenly she was living the kiss she'd wanted so desperately last night.

It started out hard and hot and insistent, his mouth plundering hers, taking her breath away.

His deep, musky scent filled her nostrils. His body heat drew her closer. Her nipples tightened and an ache started between her legs. And she couldn't help herself. She leaned into him, molding herself to his hard frame despite the crowd of people that stood just on the other side of the potted palm. The laughter and music faded until she only heard the pounding of her heart, and there was just the two of them and the kiss.

One that quickly morphed into something softer and more persuasive when she wrapped her arms around his neck and angled her head to give him better access. His arms slid around her waist, drawing her even closer. His tongue swept her bottom lip and dipped inside, stroking and coaxing and drawing a raw moan from deep in her throat.

It was a kiss like no other, and just when she was really getting into it, he drew back.

He stared down at her, his breathing hard, his blue eyes dark and unreadable, as if he couldn't quite believe what had just happened. The look faded quickly, however, into a hard, glittering light.

"You asked for a kiss—there you go. Objective achieved."

*If* that had still been her objective.

It wasn't, she realized as she stood there, her lips tingling and her nipples aching and her body on fire. She was no longer the same awkward seventeen-year-old who'd stared across the desk at the cutest boy in high school and fantasized about feeling his lips on her own.

She was all grown-up now, and her fantasies went way beyond a chaste kiss. Even more, she didn't shy away when it came to something she wanted, be it the next job promotion or a new, trendy sofa or a man. Even this man.

*Especially* this man.

Because he was everything she'd ever wanted in a man and she'd left town without ever touching or tasting him. Because she'd been scared of rejection. A fact that had haunted her all these years.

Well, no more.

When she rolled out of Cadillac this time, she would have no regrets. She would face her fear and turn her hottest fantasy into a reality.

"Not quite 'objective achieved'."

"What do you want from me?"

"Just once I want to know what it would feel like." She licked her lips and stared into his eyes. "You and me and sex. Some down-and-dirty, hot-and-heavy *sex*."

# 5

MADELINE PULLED up in front of the two-story white farmhouse with the wraparound porch, killed the engine and barely ignored the urge to whack her forehead against the steering wheel.

Instead, she drew in a deep breath and tried to calm her pounding heart.

Pounding, even though it had been over an hour since she'd propositioned Austin Jericho.

She truly wanted one night of hot, breath-stealing, mind-blowing sex with him to prove she truly had evolved into a fearless female who lived life rather than dreamed about it.

But wanting it and actually *saying* it were two very different things.

That explained her frantic heartbeat.

That, and the fact that she had a hankering for a colossal piece of wedding cake that no amount of carrot sticks dripping in fat-free dressing could begin to curb. Add to that the fact that she was stuck back in her hometown for the next two weeks with a dog who shed and an obnoxious uncle. Talk about stress.

On top of everything, the aforementioned obnoxious uncle was now MIA.

She still couldn't believe it. One minute she'd spotted him scarfing up pigs-in-a-blanket and sweet-talking Gertrude Meyers who'd made the pigs, and then—poof!—he was gone.

She'd searched for him, questioning everyone at the reception and all she'd managed to discover was that Gertrude had listened to his proposition and then promptly smacked him on the nose with an unwrapped weenie.

That was the last anyone had seen of him.

"Please let there be a message," she murmured as she struggled from behind the wheel—not an easy feat for a woman wearing yards of bright coral taffeta and tulle. She gathered the skirt and started for the door.

With any luck, he'd called and left word that he was over at the bingo hall or midnight bowling over at Cadillac Alley.

If not…

She forced the negative thought aside, squared her shoulders and mounted the porch steps. She was proactive. A doer, not a dreamer or a worrier. While the evening hadn't gone exactly as planned—she'd lost Uncle Spur and been turned down by Austin—she would make the best of it. She would find the obnoxious old man *and* seduce one stubborn cowboy right out of his Wranglers and into her bed.

Her mind made up, she spent the next five minutes checking the answering machine and casing the house. Upstairs, she peeked in to make sure his luggage was still there. Bingo. She bypassed Sharon's old room and picked up her steps, eager to dispel the sudden emptiness that spread through her.

Worry soon followed as she finished her search and came up empty-handed. Her mind raced and she envisioned the old man lying in a ditch somewhere, possibly hurt and mangled and—

*Think positive.*

*Think Austin.*

She could still see the hungry light in his eyes, feel the tension in his muscles as he'd held her during the dance.

He was being more stubborn than her lucky burner back at the lab. It was so old and corroded that she had a heck of a time lighting it, but she always managed. It was just a matter of turning up the heat and being persistent.

That's exactly what she had to do with Austin. Turn up the heat between them and tempt him beyond reason. Until his resistance melted away and he burned as fiercely for her as she did for him.

Downstairs, she penned a quick note for Uncle Spur that said "Stay put." She grabbed her purse, walked back outside and turned to pin the note on the door.

Of course, she wasn't exactly sure how to light Austin's fire. She'd used all of the usual seductive tricks last night. She'd been bold and forthright, and made it obvious she was no longer the same chubby hometown girl who'd stammered and blushed and hidden behind homemade flower-print dresses and jumbo blueberry muffins. She'd worn a daring top and a tight skirt and told him about her life in Houston. She'd smiled and licked her lips and plastered herself against him just the way she'd seen women do at the clubs in Houston. The few clubs she'd actually been to, that is. Despite her best efforts, he'd still walked away.

"This is going to be much harder than I thought," a deep, crackling voice sounded just to her left.

"You're telling me—Uncle Spur!" Her gaze swiveled to the dark shadow that sat on the porch swing and her hand faltered on the note. Spur's balding head glittered, reflecting a ray of moonlight and illuminating his weathered face. The smoke from his cigar curled in the air.

Relief washed through her. "I've been looking everywhere for you."

"Didn't see you look here. This is where I've been sitting for the last half hour. Saw you whiz right past me like a giant orange pumpkin with legs."

"Why didn't you say anything?"

"You had your mind set on something and I didn't want to distract you."

"I had my mind set on you." She pinned him with an accusing stare. "I looked everywhere at the reception."

"I ain't at the reception."

"But you *were* at the reception. You were chasing Gertrude."

"I wasn't chasing anybody. That woman wanted *me*."

"She slapped you with a weenie."

"Purely accidental. She was playing hard to get. She wanted me, but I ain't one for games, and I sure as hell cain't survive on a few measly weenies wrapped in biscuit mix. I need some real food, and that woman can only do finger food. Had to break her heart and move on to greener pastures. Emmaline Waller.'' He let out a low whistle. ''Now there's a filly who can cook. Won the corn-bread cook-off last year over in Austin County.''

''Emmaline Waller? The lady who owns the fruit stand next to Skeeter's Drugstore?''

''That's the one. Has a walking cane shaped like a giant banana. Right nice lady even if she ain't much of a looker. Anyhow, I was going into the men's room on account of that dadblamed weenie squirted juice and stained my favorite Sunday shirt. Emmaline offered to help get the stain out, and I knew right then and there that she was The One. Proposed to her between the sink and the urinals. I told her I had a two-hundred-square-foot kitchen with every major appliance and a year's supply of Viagra, and if she played her cards right, she might be the lucky lady who gets to try both.''

''Sounds romantic.''

''That's what she said right before she whacked me on the head with that dadblamed banana.'' He eyed her. ''You ought to try a few bananas. They might help shrink them hips of yours.'' He squinted his eyes. ''Then again, from the look of 'em, it'll take a lot more than a piece of fruit. More like an act of God.''

''I can see why Emmaline whacked you.''

He frowned. ''She's crazy is all, but I ain't gonna be discouraged. First thing tomorrow, I'm headed down to the diner." He wiggled his eyebrows. "The senior ladies do Sunday breakfast there afore church. While she's out of the running—too dangerous—there should be plenty others to choose from."

"But you fly home tomorrow morning."

"No sirree. I ain't going home empty-handed." He stood and walked toward the front door. "Don't just stand there. I need my beauty sleep." He waited while she unlocked the door before preceding her inside. "But first I need my nightly buttermilk." He headed to the kitchen.

Madeline flicked the light switch back on and a warm yellow glow pushed back the shadows in the living room.

Cheryl Louise and her new husband had opted to move in here rather than find a place of their own, and so all the furniture still sat in the exact spot Madeline remembered from all those afternoons spent studying here with Sharon.

Recliner near the TV. Sofa sitting in front of the double bay windows overlooking the front yard. Dining room off to the left, complete with a china hutch overflowing with rose-patterned dinnerware. Of course, Cheryl Louise's family had never owned a dog and so the massive amount of dog hair coating the sofa and rug, the fabric recliner, even the coffee table, were new to the house.

Otherwise, everything was exactly the same.

Even Sharon's room.

Not that she'd been inside. But the closed door still sported the same Madonna poster, along with a handmade Keep Out sign in bright pink bubble-shaped letters. She and Sharon had posted the sign after being interrupted while watching a rerun of *Dukes of Hazzard.* The show and the star, handsome Bo Duke, had needed their utmost concentration.

Madeline drew in a deep breath, suddenly feeling restless. Thinking solved nothing. She refused to think about the past. She had to live for the moment. Sharon's death had taught her that.

*"I don't know about you, Maddie, but I want to do something with my life. I want to go places and see things and be somebody."*

Growing up, Madeline had never really felt the same urge that had monopolized her friend's thoughts and conversations.

Correction—Madeline had never *acknowledged* the urge. While she'd dreamed of bigger and better things, she'd never imagined them as real possibilities. They'd been dreams. Pie-in-the-sky, unattainable fantasies of a small-time girl in a small-time world. In real life, she'd never considered a future beyond Cadillac and her family's business. Sure, she was smart. But she'd meant to use her intelligence to help Sweet & Simple grow and prosper. She'd never thought beyond mixing up a new muffin flavor, or perfecting a quadruple-chocolate-chunk brownie.

That had been her future. To be the Betty Crocker of Cadillac, Texas.

Until Sharon's death.

When Madeline had stood beside the grave, she hadn't seen the flowers or the shiny casket being lowered into the ground. Instead, she'd seen the next day, and the next, and all the days after that, and she hadn't felt the usual enthusiasm.

Instead, she'd felt the urge to move. To *go*. Here, there, everywhere until she'd seen and done so much that her small town and her past paled in comparison.

And that's just what she'd been doing.

And that's what she would continue to do just as soon as she finished her two-week sentence in Cadillac. She'd go back to the big city and straight up the corporate ladder. Make a name for herself in the high-profile cosmetics industry. Become the chief scientist for the fastest-growing company in the business.

Meanwhile, she had a date with a vacuum cleaner.

She'd just pulled the machine into the living room to suck up dog hair when Twinkles bounded in from the kitchen. The animal came at her, tongue wagging.

"How come he doesn't do this to you?" she asked Uncle Spur, who'd walked in from the kitchen, a half-empty glass of buttermilk in his hand.

"Gave him a whack with my *Reader's Digest* a few years back at Christmastime. He ain't liked me since. I'll just leave you two alone," Uncle Spur said as he started up the stairs. "Make sure to keep it down. I get downright ornery if I don't get my sleep."

She listened to the sound of fading footsteps before turning her full attention to Twinkles. She managed to get the dog calmed down enough to usher him to his doggie bed. She refilled the food and water bowls beside it and flipped on the small color TV that sat on a nearby stand.

The dog slurped at his water and wagged his tail as *Saturday Night Live* blared from the TV. With the dog busy, Madeline walked back into the living room and surveyed the damage.

The coral bridesmaid's dress she wore was now covered with hair, the same salt-and-pepper strands that littered the floor and clung to the sofa and tickled her nose and—"Achewww!"

Uncle Spur grumbled from upstairs as Madeline hit the vacuum's on button.

Ten minutes later, Madeline hauled herself upstairs and collapsed on Cheryl Louise's bed. She stared up at the ceiling and let loose a deep sigh. She should get herself upright and peel off the god-awful dress, but she needed to take a breather first. She'd been on her feet for so long and...ahhh. She kicked off her shoes and wiggled her toes. She undid the buttons of the dress and dipped her fingers into the bodice to loosen the confining strapless bra. Elastic gave way and the underwire eased. She took a deep breath and felt her breast swell against her fingertips. One finger grazed her nipple. It sprang to life and an ache shot through her.

She closed her eyes and pulled the edges of the bodice apart. Her fingertips went to her tender nipples and she rolled and plucked and imagined it was Austin's touch instead of her own.

*"You and me and sex."*

She wanted it in the worst way. She needed to expend the sexual energy whirling inside her. Otherwise, how was she going to concentrate on her work for the next few weeks? Why, she'd hardly thought about V.A.M.P. all day, much less her new project. Instead, she'd thought about Austin and all the things she wanted to do with him.

*Just once.*

That would be enough to satisfy her curiosity. To maintain her sense of pride. To prove to herself that she truly had changed from the girl she'd been so long ago.

The one who'd lied about the love note and forfeited what would have surely been the most amazing kiss of her life. Instead, she'd spent the rest of the night dreaming about it.

But this went beyond kissing now. She needed more to satisfy the ache inside her.

She let her hands fall away as she pushed to her feet. Several minutes later, she'd managed to trade the awful dress for a pair of shorts and a T-shirt. Downstairs, she headed for the kitchen and the refrigerator. She unearthed a diet cola, popped the tab and downed half the can with one swallow.

It was cold and gave her a moment of relief from the heat burning her neck and face. She sank down onto a chair at the kitchen table and glanced around the small but quaint room. Gingham curtains hung from café rods. At least a dozen fat pink pig figurines in various poses sat on a curio shelf above the sink. A matching set of pink pig canisters stood on the counter just to the left of the stove. Rows of mason jars lined the cabinets, filled with everything from pickled cucumbers to homemade jam to the familiar cherry preserves Maddie had always loved.

An image rushed at her, of two teenage girls sitting at this very kitchen table with its pink pig tablecloth, slathering muffins with cherry preserves and talking about everything from boys to big-city life.

Sharon had done most of the talking while Maddie had listened to her friend's deep longing for skyscrapers and traffic lights and people. Lots of new, different, exciting people rather than the small, familiar, boring population of Cadillac.

Her chest tightened and she struggled for a nice, easy breath as she pushed away the memory and focused on the task at hand—seducing Austin Jericho.

A task she intended to approach the way she did every other project she undertook. Formulate a groundbreaking, foolproof, step-by-step plan and stick to it until she achieved the desired results.

Her gaze lingered on the box she'd carried in earlier from her trunk. It contained the base ingredients for the new lotion guaranteed to land her a promotion from senior chemist to chief of research and development.

A lotion that still needed an edge. Something to make it stand out on the shelves and reinforce V.A.M.P.'s already seductive image in the market.

*Seductive.* As in *seduce.*

The thought rooted in her mind and an idea sparked. She bolted to her feet and paced the length of the kitchen as her mind raced. She needed a lotion that could seduce the senses. But not merely one or two.

All *five* of the senses. Something with all-around appeal.

Something completely and totally irresistible to the opposite sex.

Something no man, including Austin Jericho, would be able to resist.

"WE'RE GOING TO MAKE *what?*" Duane asked the next morning when Madeline phoned him at the lab.

"An aphrodisiac body lotion. A lotion guaranteed to seduce the five senses."

"The taste, touch and smell I get. But a body lotion you can hear and see?"

"I haven't worked out the specifics, but I'm sure it's possible."

"If you say so."

"It's a great marketing edge. No one's done it before.'

"I'm sure there's a reason for that."

"Can't never could."

"And here I thought you were a scientist when I've really been working next to a Plato wannabe."

"Would you just get online and research aphrodisiacs. Everything from smells to foods to colors purported to have seductive qualities."

At Duane's negative grumble, Madeline added, "We can do this."

"If you say so."

"It would be nice to have a little positive feedback. I thought you wanted to move up the corporate ladder?"

"I do, and we can. I hope."

"Look, I know it's a little far-fetched, but if certain products can seduce one or two of the senses, why not one that can seduce all of them?" Before he had a chance to respond, she added, "If we pull this off, I can promise you a major promotion. A bigger salary. The key to the corporate lounge."

"And a hot plate next to my workstation?"

"Since when is it necessary to heat up a peanut-butter sandwich?"

"I've traded the peanut butter for grilled-cheese sandwiches."

"Which you're making and eating in the lunch-room, right?"

"If you say so."

She started to argue, but realized there wasn't much she could do sitting over one hundred miles away. She would just have to trust Duane and hope for the best.

"E-mail me everything you can find by tomorrow morning," she told him and hung up.

Madeline turned her attention to the kitchen, where she went about setting up a temporary place to work. Once she had an operable lab, she intended to sit down with her laptop and do some research of her own. Hearing would certainly be the most difficult sense to entice with a body lotion, but it *was* possible. It was just a matter of narrowing down certain audible elements that created a stimulating response and adapting those to her product.

In the meantime, for each sensory test, she needed a test subject. A certain stubborn, pigheaded, sexy-as-sin test subject, who wore faded jeans and scuffed boots and a cowboy hat, would do just fine.

She smiled as she headed out to the car to retrieve the last of her supplies from the trunk.

Austin Jericho didn't stand a Popsicle's chance in hell.

# 6

"RELAX, HONEY, and this whole thing will go nice and easy. I promise."

Austin stroked the jittery female before he touched the ointment to the gash in the cow's side. The animal bellowed but didn't move beneath his steady hand.

"There, there. I told you it wouldn't hurt." Another bellow, but this one was softer as he stroked her a few more times and applied more medicine. "You like it, don't you? I knew you would. It's just a matter of loosening up, sugar." He continued his careful application, until he'd completely covered the wound with the antibiotic cream he'd picked up at Skeeter's.

Mabel was the fifth animal in two weeks who'd gotten caught in the barbed wire that circled his small spread. Most had been calves too naive to know better, but this one was full-grown. And hungry.

His own pastureland could no longer sustain his herd. Though he supplemented with feed, it simply wasn't enough. And he had a new shipment of heifers to accommodate.

He wiped his hands, reached for a handful of oats and held the reward out to the cow. A few cautious sniffs and a large pink tongue lapped at his palm.

When the goodies were all gone, she kept going, licking and searching.

"Now, now, sugar, don't get riled up. There's plenty more where that came from. Don't ever let it be said that Austin Jericho deprived a hungry female."

"That's exactly what I would say."

The soft, familiar drawl slid into his ears. Every nerve in his body jumped to awareness, along with a few strategic body parts.

He turned to find Maddie standing in the barn doorway. Wearing a tight white T-shirt—the words Party Princess printed in pink glitter letters across the front—and a denim miniskirt, she looked just as delectable as she had last night. The material stretched over her full breasts and rode up with each breath she took, giving him a tantalizing glimpse of her belly button just above the waistband of her skirt. A gold hoop glittered against her tanned skin.

First a tattoo, now a pierced navel. She'd definitely turned into a wild woman, and damned if the thought didn't stir up lust rather than disappointment.

"What are you doing here?" he asked her.

"Watching you sweet-talk a cow. I knew you couldn't have changed that much." She smiled. "Still trying to get your way with the ladies."

He grinned. "I stick to the four-legged kind now. They're much easier to please." He gave the cow another handful of oats before exiting the stall. "Low maintenance. An easy hand and a little food and they're happy."

"I like an easy hand myself."

The words echoed through his head, confirming what he already knew to be true. Maddie had, indeed, changed.

After a near-sleepless night tossing and turning and replaying her words at the reception, he'd thought that maybe he'd dreamed the entire thing.

But standing here in the bright light of day, staring at the attractive woman, hearing her words, he knew it had been no dream.

Maddie was a one-night stand just waiting to happen. Dangerous to his peace of mind. And completely off-limits.

He frowned. "I really don't have time to visit. I've got work to do."

"So do I. I didn't come to visit. I'm here in the name of science and high-priced cosmetics. I need an objective opinion on this new product I have in the works. I'm trying to decide between several different scents and I thought you could help."

"Why me?"

"This product is for women."

He grinned. "Last time I looked, I wasn't even close."

"It's for women to wear to attract men. It's pleasing to the opposite sex and since you're a member of the opposite sex..."

"So is everyone down at the Elks Lodge."

"I need someone under sixty-five."

"That leaves over half the patrons of Cherry Blossom Junction."

"Minus two-thirds who are either perverted, clueless or married. I need a normal, single red-blooded American male who knows women. A guy who's been with women. A guy who's experienced. If my lotion can entice an experienced man such as yourself, then it's sure to work on the not-so-experienced man.''

''There's the weekly football party down at the Pink Cadillac. Most of those guys are from the old jock set and at least three or four are single. Some four or five times over, but then you do want experienced.''

''And not a one of them owes me a favor.''

''And I do?'' At her nod, he added, ''How do you figure?''

''Tutoring lessons every day after school for our entire senior year. That's over two hundred hours of my valuable time.''

''You volunteered.''

''I was coerced by Miss Marshalyn.''

''Well, so was I.''

''Then we're even there. I gave my time, you gave yours, but you got something back. You aced algebra. What did I get?''

He grinned. ''The pleasure of my company.''

''Contrary to what you and your massive ego might think, it wasn't all that pleasurable for me.'' She eyed him, her green eyes twinkling. ''But it could be.''

''Don't even think what you're thinking. I've got my mind set on something permanent. I'm settling down.''

''Today?''

''Well, no.''

"Then you can stop by Cheryl's place tonight and help me out."

"I don't think so."

She gave him a pointed stare. "You wouldn't have graduated if not for me and my tutoring. Look, I'm on a time limit. I don't want to waste it looking for another test subject."

"I've got cattle to tend. I don't have a lot of free time."

"I didn't either back then, but I made time."

She had a point. Silence stretched between them for several long moments. "If I did manage to drop by, not that I'm going to, what would I have to do?"

"I'll be perfecting my product over the next two weeks while I'm dog-sitting. You'll be my guinea pig. I'll create different variations. You'll sample them, be it by taste or smell or touch, and give me your opinion. It's that simple."

"Just sampling?"

"Just sampling."

"No funny business?"

"No funny business." At his pointed stare, she added, "Just what kind of a girl do you think I am?"

"The dangerous kind."

She beamed. "Okay, so maybe I am. But I swear I won't rip off your clothes and jump your bones." She said the words, but he didn't miss the look in her eyes. A look that told him to watch out because he would be the one ripping off her clothes and jumping her bones before all was said and done. "Girl Scout's honor."

"You were never a Girl Scout." He eyed her. "Come to mention it, why weren't you a Girl Scout? You would have made a perfect Girl Scout."

She glared at him before shrugging. "They met on Saturdays and that was always one of the busiest days at the doughnut shop. My dad needed me."

"But if they'd met on a different day, you would have been right there. The leader of the pack. Ugly outfit and all."

"I would not have worn that ugly outfit."

"You lived for outfits like that."

"What's that supposed to mean?"

"That you were always wearing those big, roomy sacks for dresses. Come to think of it, why did you wear those?"

She looked ready to tell him to take a flying leap, but then her anger seemed to fade as she shrugged. "My mother made them. She thought I liked them."

"Did you?"

"I appreciated them. She put a lot of effort into making my clothes. Sewing was her passion. I didn't want to hurt her feelings, so I wore everything without complaint. She was still making things for me up until a few years back. I bought her a pottery wheel for Christmas and, just like that, the sewing stopped. It seemed she liked the new hobby more and I haven't seen any more dresses since. Just plates. And bowls. And mugs. I have an entire handmade collection."

"You should have bought her one a lot sooner and saved everyone at Cadillac High a lot of eyestrain."

She glared at him again before a smile lifted the

corner of her mouth. "They were pretty bad, weren't they?"

"Not bad as in ugly. Bad as in too much. I always wondered what you looked like underneath all that fabric."

Surprise flashed in her brilliant green gaze, followed by a warm light that revved his heart almost as much as the sight of her in her tiny white princess T-shirt.

"I never thought—" she started, but he jumped in, determined to steer them back onto a safer path.

"Would you look at the time?" He glanced at his watch and gathered up his supplies. "I've got an entire shipment of new heifers in the branding pen." He exited the stall and did his damnedest to ignore the sweet scent of her that followed him toward the tack room. "I'll see you tonight."

"Maybe. I've got a load of fence down on the west stretch and that'll take a good couple of hours to mend after the branding's done."

"Just make sure you're done by eight. I'll have the first test sample ready then."

He was *not* going to show up.

That's what Austin told himself as he watched her walk away, her round bottom swaying to and fro beneath the faded denim.

The past was just that—the past. A long time ago. While she might have helped him out, he couldn't return the favor. He was busy—busier than she'd ever been with her studying and baking way back when. This was his life. His land. His future.

One that didn't include Madeline Hale.

He had cattle depending on him. Not to mention several ranch hands. And Miss Marshalyn. She expected him to make good on his promise and settle down with a serious marriage prospect in time for her party just a couple of weeks away.

Then again, he'd depended on Maddie and she'd been there for him when he'd needed her the most. She'd been right. He wouldn't have graduated without acing algebra. And he wouldn't have aced the class without Maddie.

Okay, so he *might* show up. If he finished with all of his work in time. But he wasn't staying very long, and he certainly wasn't going to have sex with her.

No matter how much he wanted to.

HE'D STOOD HER UP.

Madeline stared at the row of saucers, each adorned with a generous dollop of the various scented compounds she'd cooked up that afternoon.

The first scent was all about hot-blooded, full-bodied femininity. It portrayed power, passion, force and heat, or so she hoped. It was a sensual berry aroma warmed with a hint of lily and jasmine that hovered between a rich floral and an oriental.

Number two relied on the old saying the way to a man's heart is through his stomach. The scent was a concoction of sweet, sensual vanilla, candied apples and cinnamon that reminded her of a rich, succulent spice cake.

Number three was a walk on the dark side with a deep, rich musk as its base. Amber and myrrh had been added and the result was positively hypnotic, or so she hoped.

Scent four leaned toward a light, playful floral, while scent five was more a fruity sorbet. All of them were stirring, and guaranteed to heat a man hotter than Texas asphalt at high noon.

If said man ever showed up.

She walked back into the kitchen and chugged half a can of diet cola before eyeing the unopened bag of Oreos. Just one, she told herself as she reached over and grabbed the goodies. To help her calm down.

*Hey, even a weight-conscious woman needed comfort food sometimes.*

Five cookies later she forced her fingers to close the bag. Her heart still raced and her nerves still buzzed, the condition even worse, thanks to the chocolate. But at least her taste buds were sated. For the moment.

Her gaze went to the laptop sitting nearby, flanked by a stack of computer notes. Several laboratory burners were scattered on the ceramic-tile countertop. Petri dishes sat here and there. An expensive, state-of-the-art microscope stood tall and proud in the far corner near a pink pig cookie jar.

While she was every bit the serious, dedicated scientist now, with the way she felt at this moment she might well have been just a wannabe back in high school.

She found herself pulled back in time to a similar moment when she'd sat in the library, her algebra book in front of her, a muffin in her hand. Excited voices had carried from the hallway as kids headed to band practice and cheerleading practice and the myriad of other after-school activities. Meanwhile Maddie Hale had waited. And waited.

Austin had failed to show up at their first scheduled tutoring session. The meeting had slipped his mind, or so he'd later told her. He'd forgotten, after she'd tossed and turned all night, anticipating the day ahead. The one hour she would spend sitting across from Cadillac's most notorious bad boy.

She'd picked out her best dress and taken extra pains with her hair, and all to sit alone in the library for an hour and a half before finally giving up.

Now she stared down at the red strapless dress she'd slipped on after a long, hot shower earlier this evening. The material clung to every inch of her ample body, revealing every curve, every bulge.

She forced aside the last thought. Twenty pounds lighter, she'd lost the bulges. *Curves* were the only thing left now, and she had plenty. The dress hugged her body, leaving little to the imagination, but then that was the point. She wanted to be a little bit outrageous.

That's why, several weeks ago, she'd walked into Eye Candy, the upscale Houston boutique that specialized in clothing like you'd find at Frederick's of Hollywood, and forked over an obscene amount of money for their top-of-the-line piece. She'd wanted to make sure that no man who pushed her lust-o-meter into the danger zone would overlook her ever again. As Austin Jericho had done twelve years ago.

The thing was, while she'd met many men, none of

them had ever pushed her into the danger zone, and so she'd yet to put the dress to the test. Until tonight. But with a few strategically placed pieces of Velcro, not to mention some hidden zippers, she had no doubt the outfit would deliver on its promise. *Sexy and irresistible.*

Add a pair of three-inch slut shoes, and she was good to go in the seduction department.

Now all she needed was the man.

Unfortunately, it looked as if history was repeating itself. A deep breath blew past her lips. At least she'd smartened up some in the past twelve years. She'd given Austin the benefit of the doubt an hour and a half before facing the truth back in high school.

But now... She checked the clock. After forty-five minutes she was calling it quits.

"Looks like you're on your own," she murmured to herself. *Again.*

"I know the feeling, gal."

Madeline glanced up to see Uncle Spur standing in the kitchen doorway, his hat in his hand, a frown on his face. A gurgle sounded and she grinned.

"You sound hungry."

He rubbed his belly. "Huntin' for a wife is hard work. I had barbecue over at the diner for lunch with a nice little filly by the name of Myrna Beth Standley, but I ain't had nothin' since on account of a little mishap."

"Would that be *the* Myrna Standley? The preacher's mother? Don't tell me you propositioned Pastor Standley's mother."

"I did no such thing. She propositioned me."

"She asked you to marry her?"

"Hell's bells, no. She propositioned me, girlie. As in *s-e-x,*" he said, spelling the last word.

"No way." At his vigorous nod, she added, "She just came out and asked you? Just like that?"

"Right there between the barbecue sandwich and the homemade onion rings."

"What did you say?"

"I told her no can do since I left my Viagra back at the ranch, and I ain't even one-hundred-percent sure it works since I haven't actually tried it yet. I'm sure it will, mind you. It's just a matter of getting the right dosage. Anyhow, I told her I'm looking for a wife not a one-night stand."

"What did she say?"

"That got her all the more revved up 'cause I said one night, which she took to mean *all* night. So she kept after me, scooting across the seat and rubbin' my leg underneath the bench. I finally had to call for help, which wasn't too easy considerin' I was wheezing something fierce 'cause I couldn't breathe. She's a big woman and she was taking up all my space. The sheriff came and threw her in the pokey and I spent all afternoon filling out an incident report so he could keep her there and teach her a lesson."

"You're pressing charges against the pastor's wife?"

"Damn straight. A man my age could have had a heart attack from all that rubbing. She's dangerous." He leaned down and picked up one of the saucers. His nostrils flared as he took a whiff. "Lordy, Lordy, I ain't smelled a good vanilla pudding in a helluva long time."

"It's a mixture of water, propylene glycol, corn-starch and magnesium silicate."

"That a fancy name for vanilla pudding?"

"It's the primary base for my new lotion."

He raised his eyebrows. "Looks like vanilla pudding."

"It's the cornstarch and the propylene glycol. They give it a full-bodied appearance."

He took another whiff. "Smells like vanilla pudding."

"It's scented with vanilla. I added a few drops to a mixture of sandlewood and jasmine, which I then added to the odorless gel. The result is a sweet, sugary fragrance."

He dabbed a finger and touched it to his lips. "Tastes like vanilla pudding."

"Don't—" she began, but he'd already fingered a huge dollop and plopped it into his mouth.

"Mighty tasty, indeed." He reached for a spoon. "'Course, it ain't anywhere near my granny's pudding. Lordy, but that woman could cook."

"It's just for testing the scent. I haven't converted to an all-edible base yet."

He spooned another bite. "She was a looker, too, back in her day." He pointed his spoon at her. "Not an ounce of extra baggage on her hips, even after three boys. She could spit, too. That's where I inherited my natural talent the likes of which the Waller County

Spit-Off ain't seen in a long, long time. 'Cept for my two brothers, that is. They inherited the talent, too, and carried on the winning tradition once I retired from the sport.''

"Cheryl Louise said they beat you and took over, which forced you into retirement."

"That gal ain't playing with a full deck." He glared before turning his attention back to the lotion sample. "Anyhow, it's no wonder I'm talented, and as fit and trim as a man half my age. It's just good breeding."

"You really shouldn't—" she said as he spooned in another heaping mound.

"Why, you would never have seen my granny lollygagging around with all these fancy schmancy machines." He pointed to her microscope and the row of burners and petri dishes. "She did everything the old-fashioned way. With lots of elbow grease. She wasn't like the women today, all spoiled and pampered." He gestured around the kitchen again. "No wonder you cain't shed that extra baby fat."

"I'm not trying to shed anything anymore. I'm all about preventative maintenance."

"You could take a lesson from a real prime specimen of a ladies' man like myself. Lose the fancy dress and get yourself some work pants and a nice, comfortable shirt. That way you can move around, get a little exercise, work up a sweat."

"I'm not trying to sweat. This is a project for work. Speaking of which, you really shouldn't eat that." The danger of consumption had become apparent when Duane had mistaken one of her gelatinous bases for raspberry yogurt. Another reason for the no-food rule now in place in her laboratory. According to Duane, the gel had worked like a triple dose of fiber. "This stuff is not ready for consumption."

"That's what you need, gal," he went on as if he hadn't heard her warning. "A little sweating and you'll work off all your extra weight in no time."

Madeline drew in a deep breath and did her best to keep from reaching up and grabbing Uncle Spur by his white pearl buttons.

"And those shoes," he went on in between mouthfuls. "Ain't a woman alive could cross a pasture wearing those things. It's no wonder the weight's just sitting there."

She smiled and picked up another saucer. "Here, try this one. It's plum."

"Mighty obliged, gal." He grabbed the other saucer and headed up to his room. "If the pastor calls, tell him I ain't here. He's been hounding me ever since he found out his ma was in the pokey. And if the sheriff calls, tell him I'll be in first thing tomorrow to finish the rest of that dadblamed paperwork. A man can only write so fast…" His words faded along with the steady thud of his boots.

Madeline glanced at the clock again and bypassed the three remaining saucers in favor of the Oreos sitting on the kitchen counter.

She took a bite of cookie number six and ignored the urge to cry. She wasn't getting all teary eyed over an insensitive jerk who didn't know a good deal when it stared him straight in the eye. So what if Austin

Jericho didn't want to have sex with her? It wasn't like he was the sex guru, or anything.

Okay, so in Cadillac he was definitely considered a guru, but in the rest of the world?

Her mind rushed back to their kiss and her lips tingled. Okay, so he might even qualify as a world-class guru. But that was still no reason to cry.

Now, a bunion and pinched toes stuffed into shoes that could double as torture devices…there was a reason to shed a few tears.

Another cookie and she wobbled upstairs. A few minutes later, she slid off her slut shoes and shoved her feet into a pair of furry bunny slippers. Fuzzy warmth welcomed her and she breathed a sigh of relief. Being seductive eye candy required a high tolerance for pain.

She felt her eyes burn and reached for another Oreo. Chocolate ecstasy exploded in her mouth, sending a flood of comfort through her body. She blinked and reached for the straps on the dress. The doorbell shrieked from downstairs and her hands paused.

Her heart jumped excitedly for a few frantic moments before reality settled in. No doubt it was the sheriff wanting more information on the pastor's mother. Or worse, maybe it was the pastor come to have it out with the "prime specimen" of eighty-something man that snored loudly from the room down the hall.

The snoring didn't even pause when the doorbell screamed again. Madeline shook her head and started downstairs, her heart pounding.

Pounding? She had to get a grip. Hadn't she learned her lesson all those years ago? It had been over an hour. It couldn't be him.

While *she'd* changed in the past twelve years—and she was wearing the dress to prove it—*he* was still the same guy he'd been back in high school. He was hot and handsome and completely uninterested in Maddie Hale.

And he was standing at her front door.

# 7

SHE WAS PRACTICALLY NAKED.

The thought registered in Austin's brain the moment Maddie opened the door.

The dress was short and tight, cut down to there and up to here. Red spandex hugged her voluptuous curves and left little to his already overactive imagination. And where there wasn't red, there was skin.

His gaze shifted up before sweeping back down. At least, he tried for a clean sweep, but his attention seemed hell-bent on pausing at several interesting spots along the way.

The smooth column of her throat. The frantic beat of her pulse. The bare curve of her shoulder. The deep swell of her breasts. The press of her ripe nipples beneath the thin material of her dress. The flare of her hips. The long, bare legs that seemed to go on endlessly.

*Practically naked, but not completely. All the major parts were covered. It wasn't as if she'd opened the door wearing nothing but a ride-me-cowboy smile.*

"You're here," she blurted as if the fact surprised her. Her full breasts heaved and the dress tugged and his heart stalled. "I mean..." She licked her lips as if fighting for her composure, then pinned him with a stern expression. "You're late."

"Another calf got caught in the west fence."

Her sternness faded into compassion. "I hope it's okay."

"She's fine. A little scratched up, but nothing some liniment couldn't fix." That and an extra hundred acres.

He focused on the thought and forced his attention away from her chest. His gaze lifted and collided with hers, and damned if the lush green of her eyes didn't take his breath away almost as much as the sight of her voluptuous body in the skintight dress.

Almost.

But Austin was a bad boy from way back. Not the sort of man to be undone by a pair of green eyes, even if they did remind him of a soft bed of freshly watered grass.

"I'm not too late, am I?" He eyed her again. "You're not heading out?"

"Out?"

"On a date." He frowned, the notion bothering him a hell of a lot more than it should have considering he had no serious intentions where Maddie was concerned. "You look like you're on your way to meet someone."

"I do?" She glanced down. "You mean this old thing?" She shook her head. "I always dress like this when I'm working."

"It's a little revealing for your line of work."

"Actually, it's perfect. Being minimally dressed

tends to keep my senses on alert, and what I do is all about the five senses.''

He gave her a suspicious look. ''It's not going to work. I'm not sleeping with you.''

''Actually, sleeping isn't what I had in mind.''

''You know what I mean.''

''If you mean sex, just say sex.''

''Okay, I'm not having sex with you. No way. No how. It's not happening. You're not my type.''

''If that's true, then it shouldn't matter what I'm wearing.''

''It doesn't matter.''

''Then why are you so worried about it?''

''I'm not.'' He shrugged. ''I hate red is all. It's my least favorite color and I wouldn't want to be distracted by my least favorite color when you probably need all of my attention for this sampling thing. So are we going to do this or not?''

''Come on in while I head out to the kitchen and get another batch of samples ready.''

''What happened to the first ones?''

''Uncle Spur ate them. Well, only two of them. It won't take long to whip up another batch of each.'' She shifted again, her long fingers playing at the doorknob as if she weren't standing there tempting him in a sexy little red number and a pair of white bunny slippers....

His gaze dropped and, sure enough, her feet sported pink bunny ears, a pink nose and long black whiskers.

''Nice shoes.''

"What?" Then she looked down at her feet and her cheeks fired a bright red.

"Do those stimulate the five senses?"

"Yes. No. Sort of." She ditched the shoes behind the door, revealing delicate feet and red-tipped toes. "They, um, relax me."

"Meaning you're nervous?"

"Why would I be nervous?"

"Because I'm here and you want to have sex with me." Funny how the word came easier when he took the offensive.

"Sex does not make me nervous."

"But I do."

"Once upon a time, maybe. But not anymore." He had the feeling she said the words more for her own reassurance than his. "I'm just tense because of work. I've got a lot riding on this new product."

"Then let's get to it." He referred to the testing, but damned if the word *it* didn't bring to mind a completely different image.

One of Madeline all soft and sweet with her sexy red dress bunched around her waist. Madeline reaching up, sliding her arms around his neck, her silky thighs parting, welcoming him inside her wet warmth for a hard, deep stroke.

His eyes locked with hers and it was as if she read his mind. Her eyes rounded and he glimpsed the old Maddie. Even more, he heard her in the sudden tremble of her voice.

"After you." She pulled open the door and motioned him inside. With a quick "Be right back," she disappeared into a doorway leading from the foyer.

He walked into the small living room, his boots slapping the hardwood floor. He stared at the wall of photographs, and his eye caught on a large framed portrait of two small girls, one holding a beat-up brown teddy bear. In the photo, Cheryl Louise had the same white-blond hair she still had. Her older sister Sharon was a direct contrast, with her thick, dark hair and even darker eyes.

His focus shifted to another picture, the girls a few years older. Then another and another before zeroing in on a small photograph of two teenage girls, books clutched to their chests as they stood in front of the science building. He'd seen Sharon hundreds of times while growing up. They'd attended the same elementary school. The same junior high. The same high school. She'd been a permanent fixture, just like the brown-haired girl who stood next to her.

He stepped closer, peering at Madeline in one of her familiar flower-print dresses. She had the same dimples she had now, the same expressive eyes, the same full lips. The package was the same, but the force inside seemed completely different.

Bolder.

More provocative.

*Dangerous.*

At least to a man who'd vowed off one-night stands and gone without sex for over six months. For him, there'd be no more hot, sweaty, forget-your-name sex. Like the sort he was sure to have with sweet Madeline.

*Easy there, Hoss.*

He drew in a deep breath and tried to ease the sudden pounding of his heart. "Nice picture," he said when he heard her moving around the dining room to his left.

"Sharon's mom took that right after we won the science fair our freshman year," she said as she walked up beside him. "We made glue out of all-natural ingredients—honey, flour, cooked sugar. It wasn't such a big deal except that it formed a nearly unbreakable bond of atoms when the concoction reached a certain temperature."

"Like superglue?"

"Supercement. I bet Mr. Vincent is still trying to get that stuff off his counter. Anyhow, we made a mess, but we also won. We actually had a write-up in the national science journal because of it. I was thrilled about the discovery, but Sharon was more jazzed about the picture that went with the article. Exposure, she called it." At his questioning glance, she added, "She liked getting all dressed up and having her picture taken. She wanted to be a model."

"Sharon?"

"I know she seemed very plain-Jane to everybody in town. It's hard to change your image with people who've watched you go through baby fat and braces and bad haircuts. But she had really great features."

He zeroed in on the picture again, and for the first time, he noted Sharon's high cheekbones and nice smile. She was pretty, all right, but not half as pretty as the girl standing next to her.

"She was going to move to Dallas and sign with Ultra, the biggest modeling agency in town. They book every major runway show in the Southwest." She stared at the picture and her eyes clouded. He sensed her loss even before he heard it in her words. "She never had the chance."

"What about you?"

"What about me?"

"Did you have modeling on your mind?"

"*Me?*" She shook her head. "I thought about it, but only as something that could never happen except in my head. I thought about a lot of things like that. Like being a rock star or a famous actress."

"Or the Incredible Hulk."

She turned on him, a smile on her face. "You wanted to be the Incredible Hulk?"

"When I wasn't dreaming about being one of the brothers from *Bonanza*." He nodded. "I kicked a lot of ass in those dreams."

"I know the feeling. I had this one fantasy where I could outsing and outdance Madonna. Reality-wise, I was more interested in cooking up new recipes for my dad."

He turned and eyed the display of colored saucers spread out across the dining-room table. "Looks like you're still cooking."

"In the lab. I don't get into the kitchen much anymore. I don't have time." He could have sworn he saw a flash of regret in her eyes.

"I know the feeling. I'm not much for cooking, but

I can eat. There's nothing like a bowl of candied sweet potatoes."

A wistful smile touched her expression. "Sharon's mom used to let us lick the bowl when she whipped the candied sweet potatoes the night before Thanksgiving." She shifted her attention to the photograph. "Sharon would have been so jazzed that I'm working for V.A.M.P. She lived for their lipsticks when we were teens. She would get her aunt from San Antonio to smuggle in a whole box every Christmas— V.A.M.P. isn't a brand you can find down at the Piggly Wiggly. Only in finer department stores." She smiled. "We would try on every color."

Silence settled in for a long moment before Austin asked, "You were with her that night, weren't you? The night it happened."

She didn't answer. She simply stared at the picture for a long moment.

"It was just the two of us," she finally said. "We were so excited about graduation the next day. It was the first day of the rest of our lives—that's what Sharon said. We were out riding around in her daddy's old boat of a car, talking about all the things we were going to do with our lives. Sharon was doing most of the talking—she always did the talking because she had so many things she wanted to do, and I was listening and then…" Fear flashed in her eyes and she shook her head, as if to rid herself of the sudden memory. "There's really no use in talking about it. It's over and done with."

He nodded. "Maybe. And maybe not."

Her gaze collided with his. "What's that supposed to mean?"

"That sometimes things live on inside of us. They keep going, on and on, until we say, 'Enough.' That's the way it was when my dad died. I watched them put him in the ground, but that wasn't the end of it."

He turned and stared at the photograph, but he didn't see the two smiling girls. He saw his dad and the rage and resentment that had lived and breathed in his glazed eyes. He heard the hate in his voice.

"He lived on inside my head for a good long time. I still hear him sometimes. *'You're worthless, boy. Worthless and useless, just like your mama'.'*" Not that it bothered him anymore. Not like Maddie's memories obviously bothered her. He'd come to terms with his dad's death. The old man and his opinion no longer mattered because Austin knew better.

"You're not worthless."

Even though he'd already come to know that on his own, hearing her say it sent a spiral of warmth through him.

"Not anymore."

"You never were."

He grinned. "I think your memory's a little warped, Thumper."

She cut a sideways glance at him. "My memory's just fine. You were wild, not worthless. There's a big difference. And don't call me Thumper."

"If the bunny slipper fits…"

"I hate you."

"Good. Then maybe you'll forget all about having sex with me."

She arched an eyebrow at him. "I don't have to like you to want to have sex. I just have to be turned on." She licked her lips and his groin throbbed in response.

"So do I, and I'm not."

She frowned at him before her expression eased into a challenging smile. "Not yet."

Before he had a chance to say anything, she motioned toward the dining-room table and the five saucers filled with various colored substances.

He had the sudden urge to turn and get while the getting was good. The less time he spent with Madeline Hale, the better. His head knew that, but damned if he could get his boots to turn the other way. They followed her into the dining room. Her hips swayed to and fro beneath the fitted dress and his mouth went dry.

Soon Austin found himself seated at the table, his heart beating a furious tempo as Madeline walked from one side to the other, leaning this way and that as she arranged the saucers and launched a full assault against his good intentions. She teased him with a cleavage shot, then a slow, lingering brush against one arm and then the ever-popular hair toss. All moves he'd seen time and time again. But damned if he didn't react like a hot and horny fourteen-year-old seeing his first full-grown woman in action.

"Okay," she said a few moments later as she retreated just enough to give him some breathing room.

"This is a basic sample test for smell, which means that we'll be focusing on this particular sense only."

"Just smell."

She nodded. "That means we have to eliminate as much stimulation as possible to your other senses. No seeing or hearing or touching or tasting. You need to be completely centered on this one sense. Clasp your fingers together and hold out your hands."

She lifted a red silk scarf and an image flashed in his head of Madeline wearing nothing but that single red scarf around her slim wrists. His groin tightened and he shifted in his seat, searching for some extra room in his jeans. He didn't find any, however. She was still too close. Too warm. And she smelled too good.

He held out his hands. The material surrounded his wrists and tightened. A few subtle brushes of her fingertips against his skin, and she'd tied the restraint in place. She pulled out another scarf and told him to close his eyes.

The silk scarf slithered across his eyes. Soft fingers brushed his cheek as she pulled the material tight and fastened a knot at the nape of his neck.

He'd never been blindfolded by a woman before. He preferred to feast his eyes and so he'd never opted for that little adventure. He hadn't imagined it could be as good as watching a woman get really turned-on.

But the next few moments, as she moved around him, her arm brushing his, the soft sound of her movement close by, came pretty damned close.

With his vision and his sense of touch gone, he had

only his hearing to focus on. His ears seemed to tune into every distinct sound. Her breaths just to the left of him, moving closer, closer…so close that it stirred the hair on the back of his neck, and another part of his anatomy.

He heard the clatter of plates in front of him and wondered if her arm extended around him. If she might accidentally brush him with her luscious breast when she leaned in just so….

Anticipation rippled through him and his blood rushed faster. It didn't matter that he couldn't see her. He *knew* she was there, and that she was turned-on, and it turned him on all the more.

He became acutely aware of his own body. He felt the heat of his palms. Heard the thunder of his own heart. Tasted the deprivation on his own lips. It was all he could do to sit still and wait for the sample test to begin, and pray to the Big Guy Upstairs that everything went as quickly as possible.

*Out of sight, out of mind,* he told himself.

Thanks to the blindfold, she was out of sight, and so he merely needed to push her out of his mind and focus on something else to regain his composure.

Like the way the sun felt beating down on him as he worked his cattle during a blazing hot summer. Or the pride that came from the knowledge that every inch of pastureland, every horse, every steer—they were all his.

*His.*

He tried to conjure the picture of his place, from

the two-story log cabin he'd designed and built himself to the large barn and the two adjoining corrals.

Nothing worked. He still pictured her, and he still wanted her despite her being all wrong for him, with her tight red dress and her bold, provocative words.

In fact, he wanted her *because* of those things.

He'd always been a sucker for red-hot women in the past. An addiction he'd felt certain he'd managed to kick. Until now.

"Sniff," she instructed him, her soft voice echoing in his ear, stirring his already heightened senses. "Breathe. Sniff again." She grew silent for a few moments. "Now rate the scent anywhere from one to five, five being the most appealing, and give your score out loud."

He concentrated on complying with every request. Sniff. Sniff again. Rate. Until he'd gone through the routine three different times. He was on number four when he leaned forward to sniff and his nose brushed soft, fragrant skin—

"I'm sniffing you," he blurted, jerking back and nearly toppling the chair.

"Of course."

"But I'm supposed to be sniffing the lotion."

"You are. I'm rubbing the lotion on my pulse points. Different fragrances smell different when they mingle with the body's natural pheromones. You have to smell it during the sample tests the way you would if the product were actually in use."

He hated to admit it, but it made sense. Still he was

wary. "You said smelling, no touching. I *touched* you just now."

"It's not my fault if you got too close."

"I can't see a damned thing. One minute you're on one side of me, the next you're on the other. How am I supposed to know if I'm getting too close?"

"What does it matter?"

"It matters."

"Because you're turned-on?"

He didn't miss the hope in her voice. He frowned. "Because I'm dizzy, and bumping into things just makes it worse."

"You're really dizzy?"

"Way dizzy. I'm this close to losing my dinner."

"That's not good."

"You're telling me."

"I suppose we could bend the rules just this once, in the name of good health. I wouldn't want you to get sick. I'll untie your hands. That way you can still feel things and maybe that will help you get your bearings." Her fingers went to his wrists and the scarf fell away. "But make sure to keep the contact limited. This test is supposed to focus solely on smell."

With his wrists free, he felt a small measure of control return. He drew a deep breath, then stood and reached for her arm.

"What are you doing?" she asked as he tugged her in front of him. Her soft breasts came up against his chest and her hips brushed his growing erection.

"Making sure you stay put." He slid his hands around her waist and lifted her onto the table. Dishes clattered and wood creaked as she settled into place. Reaching behind him, he felt for his chair, then pulled it up close and sank down.

There was a moment of silence before her fingers closed around his hand. She guided his touch to her neck. "This sample is right…here."

Her hand fell away as his fingertips trailed up the curve of her neck and then drifted lower. He traced the shape of her collarbone before leaning forward and drinking in her scent. Once. Twice. A third time.

"What do you think?" Her voice was breathless and soft and stirring.

"I can't think." Not with her scent filling his head and her heat seeping into his fingertips and his heart pumping so damned fast. "I don't want to think."

Right then, he wanted something altogether different.

He wasn't sure what happened in that next instant. Maybe it was the blindfold that blotted out reality and made the future he'd planned for himself seem a distant, far-off dream. Maybe six months without a woman had finally caught up to him and scrambled his common sense. Maybe both.

He didn't know. He only knew that he had to touch her. Right here. Right now.

His palms cupped the backs of her calves, his fingers curving around, molding their shape. He stroked, relishing the feel of her soft, smooth skin as he moved up, stroking the outsides of her knees, her thighs. He reached the hem of her short dress and halted, his fingers playing at the edge of the material. He smoothed his hands over the tops of her thighs and dipped inside, urging her legs apart.

Her breath caught as he touched his lips to the inside of her knee.

He licked and nibbled his way up the inside of her thigh until he reached...

"Damn, you're not wearing any panties," he growled accusingly, his lips just shy of the slick, damp folds between her legs. Her provocative scent filled his nostrils and his erection throbbed.

"I never wear panties. I mean, I do, but not with this dress. It's too clingy and tight. Even a thong shows through." Oddly enough, she sounded almost apologetic.

A crazy thought because she'd obviously changed from the girl he once knew.

He knew that, but there was just something about the tremble of her voice that made him want to believe her and chase away the sudden tension that filled her body, until all that remained was desire.

He slid his hands beneath her, cupped her bottom and pulled her to the very edge of the table.

He bit the soft flesh on the inside of her thigh, relishing her loud gasp before he touched his mouth to her. She cried out at the sudden contact. She gripped his shoulders, her fingers digging into his hard muscles.

He trailed his tongue up and down her slit. She tasted wild and ripe and he couldn't get enough. He devoured her, licking and tasting and sucking every delectable inch until she cried out, her hips thrusting against his mouth.

He pulled back then, just long enough to yank the blindfold from his eyes. She stared down at him, her green eyes wild and full of wonder, as if she'd never felt a man's mouth on her.

*As if.*

Keeping his eyes locked with hers, he reached out and slid his middle finger deep inside her before withdrawing and sliding back in. She was warm and slick and so damned tight around him. It took all of his control to keep from coming right there, but more than his own need, suddenly he wanted to fulfill hers. Because she was so turned-on and he knew by the desperation in her eyes that she needed release.

With his thumb, he pressed on her swollen clitoris and stroked. Back and forth. Up and down. The nub ripened and grew taut. Wetness flooded between her legs, easing the way for his finger that moved in and out. Soon her body tensed and her hips strained against his hand. Her lips parted on a loud moan and her eyes fired brighter, and she came apart.

The chair toppled backward when he bolted to his feet to lean over her and catch her cries with his mouth. He kissed her then. Deeply. Thoroughly. He slid one arm around her, holding her to him while he kept one finger deep inside. She clenched and unclenched around him in a delicious rhythm that made his erection throb so hard it hurt.

"I'm on fire," she murmured against his lips.

He knew the feeling. He felt ready to burst into flames himself.

"You have to do something." Her soft words were like a match to a fuse. "We have to do something."

Suddenly he couldn't move fast enough. He'd always been a man who could control himself with a woman, but just like that, he lost it. He wanted to be inside her. He needed it. And that was all that mattered.

"I want you so much I can hardly breathe," she murmured, her voice breathless.

His own breaths sawed past his lips in a fast, furious rhythm as he withdrew his hand and reached for his zipper. He was so hard that the button wouldn't budge on the first tug.

"Dammit," he growled, yanking. The metal popped off and flew across the room. He reached for his zipper. The teeth hissed open and his jeans sagged onto his hips. His thick erection sprang forward.

"I want you so much I feel dizzy," she went on, her words feeding his desperation. "And so hot."

The sensitive head of his penis brushed her slick heat and he groaned. His hand dove in his back pocket for his wallet and the condom stashed there. She grasped him, her fingers closing around his pulsing thickness, stroking. His grip on the wallet faltered.

"And my heart is pounding so fast. And so loud."

He knew the feeling. He could hear the drumming of his own heart. *Bam, bam, bam!* Followed by the voice, "Is everything all right in there—"

Wait a second. A voice?

Austin's fingers on the wallet halted as reality pushed past the lusty haze consuming his senses.

"It's pounding really loud," she murmured.

Regret washed through him. "That's not your heart, Thumper. It's the door."

"The door?"

"Someone's at the door."

"Someone's at the door?" Her eyes fluttered open and she stared past him. Her gaze widened as reality seemed to hit her. *"Someone's at the door."*

"It's Pastor Standley," a muffled voice called. "I can hear you all in there. Is everything okay?"

"F-fine. Just a minute," she called back. She frowned as she watched Austin stuff his massive erection back into his pants. "Talk about rotten timing."

"Or divine intervention."

"If that's supposed to be an 'I told you so,' save it. This is not a sign from anything higher than the second floor." At his raised eyebrow, she added, "Uncle Spur. He's pressing charges against the pastor's mother for propositioning him. I'm sure that's why he's here now."

"You can press charges for that?"

"Don't even think it. You want this as much as I do."

He eyed her a moment more. "Actually—" he pressed her hand to the bulge in his pants "—I want it more." He gave her a quick, hungry kiss before pulling back and helping her off the table.

He turned away then, leaving her to straighten her own clothes while he went to answer the door. Otherwise, he was sure to lose what little control he had, press her back onto the table and finish what they'd started.

He wanted to, but he didn't *want* to want to.

He *wanted* to concentrate on finding himself a nice, wholesome, respectable girl and winning his bet with Miss Marshalyn.

Unfortunately, the notion didn't seem half as appealing as it had before Madeline Hale had come rolling back into town, back into his life and right into his hottest fantasies.

# 8

MADELINE CLOSED the door after reassuring Pastor Standley that she would talk to Uncle Spur about dropping the charges against his mother.

She walked back over to the table and sat down. The past evening rushed through her mind, right up to the point where she'd had the best orgasm of her life.

The best, and the first when it came to oral sex. Sure, she'd been on the receiving end before. But no man had ever pleasured her to the point of explosion. The guys she'd been with had been too intent on their own pleasure, too eager to get to the actual act to hold off just for her benefit.

Austin was different. He gave new meaning to the word *foreplay* and she couldn't wait to see in what other ways he'd outperform the few lovers in her past.

Unfortunately, she was going to have to wait. He'd made some excuse about having to get up early and then left right after opening the door to Pastor Standley.

But he'd promised to be on time for their next session.

She recalled his earlier words: *"Actually, I want it more."*

A smile curved her lips as she gathered up the saucers and headed for the kitchen. While she hadn't actually seduced him—she'd been the one to have an orgasm—she'd at least driven him beyond the point of denying the attraction between them. She knew now that he truly *did* want her.

Just as she knew that he liked red, despite his earlier denial. He'd gone over the edge after sniffing sample number four—the lilies and jasmine scented with succulent berries. It was a sensual, hot-blooded, full-bodied aroma. Passionate. Racy. *Red.*

Lifting the plate, she inhaled. Her nostrils flared and her stomach fluttered madly.

This one definitely drew a major response. Then again, the others were potent, as well. As she sniffed her way through the other four saucers before depositing them in the sink, the sensations in her body didn't diminish. If anything, her blood rushed faster and her heartbeat pumped at an alarming rate. She was definitely on to something. The realization sent a rush of adrenaline through her.

She spent the next half hour cleaning the dishes, straightening her makeshift lab and making notes in her test journal. Then she headed upstairs. After peeling off the red dress, she stepped beneath a cold shower. Water sluiced over her heated skin, but it did little to ease the desire still pumping through her body.

Because she didn't just want her own orgasm. She wanted to come along with Austin. To feel him slide into her body and explode in her arms. To feel his heart pound the same fast, furious rhythm as her own.

To know deep in her heart that she was the one responsible for his orgasm. That she truly had changed into a woman that Austin Jericho couldn't resist. He was the last doubt that lingered in her mind. Her one regret.

But not for long.

Tomorrow night she would make sure there were no interruptions. Just sex. Mutually satisfying sex.

THEY WERE *NOT* GOING to have sex.

Austin told himself that for the umpteenth time later that night as he turned onto his left side and did his best to get some much-needed sleep. He clamped his eyes shut, but she was there, the memory of her in that next-to-nothing red dress, her body tight and slick around his finger, her cries of ecstasy echoing in his ears.

He opened his eyes and stared at the wall. The tree outside his window cast a shadow there, the branches trembling with a small breeze.

The temperature outside had dropped a few degrees, but it wasn't nearly enough to cool the heat that burned him up from the inside out. Even a cold shower and several glasses of iced tea had offered little relief. He was still hot. Still horny.

Still crazy.

Despite the fact that he knew Madeline was all wrong for him, he *still* wanted her. In the worst way.

He shook his head, sat up and threw his legs over the side of the bed. After yanking on a pair of jeans, he walked down the hallway of the sprawling, one-story ranch house. When he'd first built the place, he'd done it with a loan from the bank. But after a few successful years with his cattle, he'd had enough to pay off his loan. He owned it outright now. All five bedrooms with an equal number of bathrooms, a massive kitchen with fully stocked cupboards and every modern convenience, and a comfortable den complete with a gigantic fireplace.

It was all his, and it was a far cry from the ramshackle old house with the sagging porch where he'd spent his youth.

He walked into the den, over to the large window that overlooked the back forty. A small dwelling sat in the far distance, barely visible from where he stood.

But Austin didn't have to see it with his eyes. He saw it in his mind. The rotting walls, the wood completely decayed in several spots. The No Trespassing sign nailed to a tree out front. Though it stood vacant now, the place had changed little from the house he'd grown up in.

Most of the windows had been boarded up to keep the cold out. Austin and his brothers had hammered the wood into place themselves one day with nails they'd pried out of old Mr. Waller's fence. The noise hadn't even stirred their dad, who'd been snoring from the front porch where he'd passed out hours before after yelling and cussing up his usual bitter, drunken storm. He'd been as immune to the winter weather as he was to the high heat of summer. He'd felt nothing except the liquor flowing through his veins, and heard nothing, not even the cries of his three boys who'd been cold and hungry and desperate.

Austin had stopped his crying early on. Tears didn't do any good. They didn't put food on the table or make warm clothes appear or force a bitter man to give up the bottle, so Austin had stopped praying for all three. He'd stopped worrying about tomorrow and wondering why things were so messed up for him and not for the other kids in Miss Jacobs's kindergarten class.

Instead, he'd started to take what he could get. He'd eaten when he could and worn whatever hand-me-downs he'd managed to scrounge up, and he'd stayed away from his father as much as possible. He'd stopped caring about what he didn't have. He'd stopped caring, period. Because he'd never had anything to really care about.

Until he'd swiped a bucket of freshly picked apples from Miss Marshalyn's back porch and gotten himself caught. She'd hauled him into her kitchen with the intent of calling the sheriff. Instead, she'd given him a lecture about respecting other people's property, along with his first good whiff of candied sweet potatoes.

From then on, he'd been hooked. He'd started picking the apples for her and setting them on her porch in the hope that her back window would be open and he would get another whiff. After a few bucketfuls, she'd invited him inside and given him a bowl of those famous potatoes.

For a price, that is. Nothing came for free, or so

she'd told him over and over, and she'd made him whitewash her front fence in payment. The chores had started then. Every day he would show up and she would give him a new task, and an overflowing plate of supper when he finished.

Even more than the food on his plate—two-thirds of which he'd always saved for his two kid brothers— he'd simply liked sitting in her kitchen, smelling the smells of a real home and feeling the warmth from the stove.

First Miss Marshalyn had filled his belly, and later she'd filled his head. With notions that anything was possible if he worked long and hard enough. She'd even given him a taste of what it was like to actually *have* something of his own.

Austin's gaze went to the bookshelf in the far corner and the kid's faded metal lunch kit that sat on one of the shelves.

It had been a hot Sunday like any other and he'd spent the early part cutting her grass while she was at church. When she'd come home, she'd not only fed him lunch, but she'd presented him with a brand-new, gleaming red *Dukes of Hazzard* lunch kit.

To an eight-year-old boy who packed his lunch in a used paper sack—when he actually had something to pack—it was like getting a cherished toy at Christmas.

But it wasn't a gift, she'd told him. He'd earned the kit with his hard work. Even more, he'd earned the lunch she proceeded to pack for him every day thereafter—more than enough for him *and* his two brothers.

He turned his attention back to the window and the

house that sat in the distance. While Miss Marshalyn and her lunch kit had made his childhood less bleak, it hadn't really *changed* anything. It had merely slowed him down on the destructive path he'd been following.

He'd still been the oldest of the no-good, no-account, troublemaking Jericho brothers, and his father had still been the town drunk.

*Trouble.*

That's what the sheriff had called Bick Jericho every time he'd pulled the man in for public intoxication.

*"You ain't nothin' but trouble, Bick Jericho."* And since Austin, Houston and Dallas had been Bick's boys, the sheriff, and a good majority of the townsfolk, had been dead certain the brothers were no better than their old man.

While Austin, himself, had never been much for drinking, he'd grown up every bit the hell-raiser his father had been. Bitter because the world had dealt him such a shitty hand. Angry because he'd been stuck with a sorry excuse for a father.

*"Born trouble, that's what you are,"* Sheriff Gentry had told Austin the night he'd landed behind bars after totaling his souped-up Harley and nearly killing himself in the process.

He'd been roaring down Main Street, a little too reckless and much too fast, and he'd lost control. He'd crashed into the sheriff's parked car, sending it straight to that great big Chevy lot in the sky.

*"You were born one-hundred-percent trouble just like your worthless old man."*

He'd believed the sheriff, until Miss Marshalyn had shown up to bail him out. She hadn't put a price on her help that night. She hadn't bargained for good behavior. She'd simply said, "You have a choice. This—" she'd pointed to the bars "—or that." She'd pointed to the door.

She'd given him not only a choice that night, but a chance, and he'd realized then that trouble was something a man *made,* not something he *was.*

It was a choice, not a birthright, and so Austin had decided then and there never to make trouble again. Instead, he'd set his sights on making a real home for himself, and a family.

He had the home. Almost. Since Miss Marshalyn's husband, Jim, had passed away, she didn't need all that property. For Austin, it would complete his spread and give him enough size to compete with the big-boy ranches.

As for the family…any of the handful of nice, respectable women he'd narrowed his choices down to would do. All he had to do was pick one and take things to the next level by asking her out.

That's what he needed to do.

But what he wanted to do was watch Maddie Hale get all hot and flushed and make those tiny moaning sounds in the back of her throat when he licked her hot slit just so….

HE STIFFENED—in more ways than one—and sank down into a leather chair. He touched his mouse pad and watched his computer spring to life. Typing in his code, he brought up the vaccination charts on the newest additions to his herd. He needed to stay focused. To think about work and the future and the fact that he didn't have time to waste on a woman who didn't suit his needs. Particularly a woman who was so... temporary.

Maddie was out of here soon, and so it stood to reason she would only be interested in sex. But Austin wanted more. He wanted the morning after.

His head knew that. Now if he could just get a certain throbbing body part to agree.

HE WAS LATE AGAIN.

Not that it mattered. She knew he would come tonight. In more ways than one. And so she took the extra time to prepare for the evening ahead.

She touched up her fading makeup *again*.

She took yet another look at her now-drooping hair.

She watched the clock while she felt drops of sweat sliding down her bare arms, the ninety-something Texas heat and the fact that she'd been slaving away in a hot kitchen all day causing her discomfort.

Drawing in a deep breath, she adjusted her off-the-shoulder, red lace tank top. Sexy and alluring had been the idea when pulling on the outfit over two hours ago. Instead, she'd wound up damp and sticky. And hungry.

At least when she'd baked at her dad's shop, she'd had a whole oven of goodies to look forward to, so the experience had seemed worthwhile and rewarding. Mixing up lotions was definitely not the same.

That's the point, she told herself. She was doing something far different now. Far, *far* away from her desperately small hometown. And the result of her hard work—a promotion and a prestigious position with V.A.M.P.—would last longer than the ten seconds it took to savor a cookie or a muffin or a brownie.

She would take power and prestige over a rush of sugar any old day.

At least that's what she told herself as she sat on the sofa, her stomach grumbling and her thighs aching as she waited for Austin Jericho.

She blew out a deep breath and busied herself rearranging the test samples. Each one had been formulated to create a different sensation upon contact with the skin. The first tingled, the second tickled. Number three heated, while four cooled. A fifth had the wet, slick feel of water.

Then again, she could do the tickle first, then the tingle. Next the cold, then the hot. Water last.

Or cold first. Hot. Tingle. Tick—

The thud of footsteps on the porch stalled her thoughts. She bolted from the couch, her heart pounding as if she'd just discovered the fountain of youth itself.

*Hel-lo?* She was a grown woman. She'd dated men. She'd touched. She'd hugged. She'd kissed. She'd even slept with a few. She wasn't a shy, overweight, nerdy Chem Gem anymore, even if she had answered the door in her bunny slippers the night before.

Tonight she wore a pair of strappy sandals with a thick heel that made her arch her back just enough when she walked to give her breasts more perk and her bottom a nice lift.

"You're late," she blurted several moments later as she opened the door. Her annoyance took a temporary vacation at the sight of him.

He filled up the front porch, looking so tall and dark and handsome in nothing but a simple black button-up shirt, the cuffs rolled up to his elbows, faded jeans and worn cowboy boots. He smelled of leather and soap and hot, aroused male, and her nostrils flared in response.

He pulled off his cowboy hat and ran a hand through his short, dark hair. The muscles in his arms bunched and stretched his sleeves and her breath caught.

His grin was slow and easy and so damned self-assured, as if he knew the effect he had on her. "Hello to you, too."

"Let me guess." She stepped back, motioning him inside. "Another trapped cow."

"A fence came down. I've spent all afternoon hammering up barbed wire." He followed her into the living room and perched on the edge of the sofa. He eyed the display of samples on the coffee table. "Looks like you had a busy day in the kitchen."

"And every other room in the house." At his questioning look, she added, "I started out on the back porch where I fed and watered the dog and the plants. Then I walked the dog. Then I bathed the dog upstairs thinking I might be able to wash off some of the extra hair. It didn't work and so I had to vacuum the upstairs and the downstairs, on account of Twinkles having raced through the house, shaking and spraying everything with water *and* hair. Then I spent a good thirty minutes trying to wake up Uncle Spur from his noon nap—he sleeps like the dead. Then another hour trying to talk him into dropping the charges against the pastor's mother—which he finally did. Then another hour convincing him to eat lunch at the diner before he went to the bowling alley to scope out women. Then I finally made it into the kitchen.''

"You sure you want to do this tonight? If you're tired—''

"Annoyed maybe, but not too tired. Not for this.'' She could tell by the way his eyes flared a bright blue that he knew exactly what she meant. "I've been waiting all day for this.''

He eyed her for a long moment, feeding the tension in the air with his hungry gaze before he sat down on the couch.

"Bring on the samples.'' He held out his hands.

"I need your hands free tonight. This is a touch test.'' She sat beside him and twisted around to reach for the blindfold draped across the back of the sofa. As she did, her nipple grazed his upper arm and sprang to life.

His eyes fixed on the reaction. He licked his lips and she knew what he wanted. To lean down, draw the tip into his mouth and tease its ripeness through the thin fabric of her blouse.

Instead, he swallowed and closed his eyes.

After last night, she'd half expected him to pin her

to the wall the moment she'd opened the front door. She'd wanted him to.

Instead, he seemed reserved.

She knew she would have to stay on the offensive and push his buttons the way she had the night before, until he was so hot and bothered that he couldn't help himself. He would respond then, and they would finish what they'd started last night. In the meantime...

She leaned into him and wrapped the satin around his face. Her breast teased him again, the friction of her nipple brushing back and forth sending a ripple of heat through her own body.

She caught a groan before it worked its way to her lips. She forced a calming breath as she walked over and turned off the radio. Silence settled in the room, disrupted only by the pounding of her own heart and the hum of the air conditioner.

She perched beside him and reached for the first sample.

"This is number one," she said. "I'm going to smooth it onto your skin. Relax and concentrate on the sensation for a few seconds. Then use three words to describe the sensation you feel."

She scooped a few drops of lotion and touched the tender skin on the inside of his wrist.

He sucked in air as she started to smooth the tingling sample over his skin, up and down, rubbing the lotion from his wrist, up the inside of his forearm. He groaned, the sound feeding the desire pulsing through her own body.

"Okay," she murmured. "Three descriptive words."

"Incredible."

"And?"

"My…" He drew in a breath. "Pulsing. I feel pulsing. Like it has a life of its own."

"No sentences. Just a descriptive word."

"Electric."

"That's good." She took a damp cloth drenched in alcohol and removed the sample from Austin's skin before leaning over and reaching for his opposite arm.

"We'll let that spot recover while we do another." She applied the next sample, her ears piqued for every nuance of sound that escaped his sensual lips.

While the lotion was supposed to be turning him on, she was the one who felt on fire. Touching him. Hearing him. Wanting him.

"This is sample two." She rubbed her fingertips against the dab of lotion, working it into his skin. Her fingers moved higher, taking the same path she'd used on the opposite arm. She smoothed the concoction along the inside of his forearm, working toward the bend of his elbow. His veins bulged, as if the blood flowed harder and faster at her touch. His arm flexed, his muscles tightening and rippling beneath her hand.

"Descriptive words," she cued, retracting her fingers and waiting for his reaction.

"Burning," Austin replied, his nerves buzzing at the warmth spreading along his skin.

Hot, yet not hot enough to be painful. Instead, it sent a wash of heat up his arm, clear through his entire body. He felt a bead of sweat slide from his temple, the moisture winding a path down the side of his face.

He'd perspired before. Hell, he spent his days outdoors in the blazing Texas heat, but he'd never really *felt* the sweat. The way it tickled along its path and wound down his jaw. His skin came alive at the sensation, along with the rest of his body. His feet flattened on the floor, his legs braced to keep himself from flipping her over and pressing her back into the sofa.

*Just give it to her and get it over with.*

That's what he fully intended to do before all was said and done.

He'd come to the conclusion early that morning, after a sleepless night spent with his books, that the only way to get back to the business of finding a potential wife was to act on his attraction to Madeline. He was spending entirely too much time and effort thinking about having sex with her. Better to do it, burn off his damned lust, and get it over with.

But while she stirred his body in a fierce way, she stirred his curiosity even more. He couldn't erase the image of her last night when she'd met him at the door in her bunny slippers. Nor could he forget the way she'd trembled and blushed when he'd stared at her a little too long. And he certainly couldn't forget the look of surprise in her eyes when he'd made her come apart with his mouth. As if he'd been the first to taste her and drive her over the edge.

He'd taken the initiative last night when she'd worked him up. Not tonight. Tonight he wanted to see just how far she would go to get him into bed. He wanted to see firsthand if she had, indeed, turned into a bona fide bad girl. Or if there was still a little of the shy, naive, wholesome Maddie hidden deep inside.

"What did you say?" she asked, her voice as soft and stirring as her scent.

"Burning." He clenched his teeth against the sensation. "Searing heat. Pure torture. Because it feels so good."

"Perfect."

Another sensation soon replaced the heat on the inside of his upper arm as he felt her soft touch again.

"Here's the next sample." Warm fingers folded the sleeve of his T-shirt up before touching another dollop to his exposed bicep. She rubbed and smoothed, working her palm against his skin, easing higher beneath the edge of his rolled sleeve and around to the sensitive underside of his arm. A tickling sensation drifted over his skin, but it didn't make him smile. Instead, he frowned, doing his best to ignore the stirring sensation.

"Descriptive words."

"It feels like you're tickling me."

"Then why aren't you smiling."

"Tickling as in teasing. *Stirring*."

He could feel her smile. "That's the response I was hoping for."

He felt the sofa shift next to him as she stood and came to sit on his opposite side. Soft hair trailed over his arm as she turned and worked at his opposite sleeve, rolling the edge up until she'd exposed his bicep.

The lotion and the rubbing soon followed, but this time he felt a coolness. Almost like the cream he rubbed into his thigh muscles after a particularly tough day working his ranch. But this sensation didn't soothe. It stirred him all the more and he barely managed a few descriptive words.

He was too worked up to talk.

He managed a colorful phrase, however, when the couch shifted again and she moved in front of him. He felt her hands on the insides of his knees. She urged his thighs apart and he had the sneaking suspicion that she'd settled on her knees between them.

''What are you doing?''

''The final sample.''

He didn't feel a dollop this time. Instead, he felt her hands on top of his, her palms slick and smooth as she slid them up his arms. Her touch pushed beneath the edges of his T-shirt to his shoulders before easing them back down.

''How does it feel?''

''Wet.'' He swallowed. ''Warm.''

''It is,'' and as she said the words, he had the distinct feeling she was referring to more than just her hands.

Her touch fell away for a few heart-pounding moments before she pushed up the hem of his T-shirt and touched his bare middle. He sucked in a breath as the slick, wet feel of her touch moved under his shirt, slicking over his abdomen and higher until her palms grazed his nipples. She rubbed the tips before trailing her fingers across his chest. Side to side, then up and down, then back to his nipples.

"Still wet and warm?"

"And hot."

"There are no heat properties in this sample."

"Not the sample. Me." He reached up and pulled the blindfold off to find his suspicions confirmed.

She was kneeling in front of him, her hands still on his chest, one covering his left nipple while the other rested against his pounding heart.

"Is this part of the sampling test?" he asked.

She eyed him, her eyes dark and glittering. "Yes—" she licked her lips "—and I really need a taste." She leaned forward and her lips closed over his right nipple. Her teeth caught him there, her tongue flicking out to ply the nub.

"Holy shit," he ground out, his gaze fixed on her head as she suckled him. Her body wedged closer, pressing against his massive hard-on and he had the sudden image of her trailing her lips lower, unzipping his pants and taking him into her mouth.

Her moist red lips pressed against his skin and he threaded his fingers through her hair, holding her close. Where her hands had felt good, her mouth felt even better, and he couldn't help himself. He'd reached his limit. He was this close to hauling her into his lap, pressing her back against the sofa and peeling her shirt away to sample her ripe nipples the way she was sampling his. He wanted to strip off her clothes and slide into her fast and furious, and end the damned attraction that had him so distracted.

And he would.

Before the evening was over he would do everything he'd been wanting to since the moment he'd seen her at Skeeter's. But first, he had to see if she was all talk and no action, or if she truly had changed.

She leaned back on her knees and stared up at him, her lips slick and parted, her eyes hungry.

"Tonight is a touch test, not a taste test," he reminded her.

"For the product. We're done with that test. This is my own private sampling of you."

His erection throbbed as her gaze dropped to his lap.

"I really want to see you." Her slim fingers reached out and she unfastened the button on his jeans. "And touch you." Her knuckles grazed him as she worked the zipper over his hard length. His entire body trembled in anticipation. He tilted up just enough to let her pull his jeans and underwear down to his hips.

His penis jutted forward from the dark patch of hair that curled around the base. The veins bulged, the skin slick and tight. Pearly liquid beaded on the ripe purple head.

"And taste you." Before he could draw a deep breath, she leaned forward, flicked her tongue out and lapped up the drop of liquid.

Heat pulsed along his nerve endings, like a flame being passed over his skin. She licked him from root to tip once, twice, making him burn hotter, before drawing him into her mouth.

He closed his eyes as a groan rumbled from deep

in his throat. Pleasure drenched his body and he braced himself against coming right then and there. He wanted this too much to have it over with so quickly. He wanted to feel her, to watch her, and then he wanted to thrust into her soft ripe body and plunge over the edge with her.

He forced his eyes open. Blond hair trailed over his lap and he reached down, pushing the soft strands back from her face so that he could see her red lips slide over his hard length. She suckled him, swirling her tongue around and around, pushing him closer to the brink until he couldn't stand it anymore.

He cupped her face and set her away from him, her confused gaze colliding with his.

"Am I doing it wrong?"

"No, darling. You're doing it right. Too right. I don't want it like this. I want to be inside you."

A smile curved her full, slick lips and she stood. She stripped off her clothes at the speed of light. He barely had time to feast his eyes on her full breasts tipped with ripe, rosy nipples before she leaned down and touched her lips to his.

He tasted his own essence on her lips and it sent a spurt of hunger through him. His tongue tangled with hers and he deepened the kiss, wanting to consume her the way she'd consumed him only a few moments ago. The kiss was hot and wet and mesmerizing. He couldn't think. He could only feel. The softness of her lips. The tantalizing dance of her tongue, the softness of her knees against his hips as she straddled him and settled over his lap.

He cupped her bottom as his penis nudged her slick flesh. Electricity shot through him, along with a burst of reality. His heart pounded double time and he gripped her bottom to keep her from sliding down.

"My pocket," he groaned against her lips, his chest heaving against hers.

"What?" Her eyelids fluttered open and he saw the confusion again. Once more he had the fleeting thought that she wasn't nearly as experienced as she pretended to be. But then she reached down between them, gripped his penis and squeezed. His thoughts scattered as pleasure gripped his senses. He barely heard her soft "Oh" past the thunder of his heart.

She let go of him then and reached for his pocket. After a few frantic seconds, she pulled out the foil packet.

After ripping open the package, she pulled out the contents and reached between them. Her fingers brushed and stroked as she slid the condom down his throbbing length. She braced her hands against his chest and then drew him deep into her body with one swift, downward motion.

The pleasure was so intense that it sucked the air from his lungs. She gripped him hot and tight. His entire body went rigid and he clenched his teeth against the exquisite sensation.

"Don't move." His hold on her bottom tightened, his fingers pressing into her softness as he held her still. "Not yet."

"I…" She licked her lips, her eyes bright with desire and a deep-seated longing that took his breath away. As if she actually felt more for him than lust.

Then she stared into his eyes and murmured, "I *have* to move." And then she did, and the only thing obvious in her expression was pleasure. Pure, exquisite pleasure.

She rode him so well, her body clasping his as she moved up and down, side to side, urging him deeper with every movement. He braced his thighs, holding himself rigid as he massaged her soft, round ass and pressed hungry kisses to her lips and throat.

The sensation mounted until he feared he couldn't take it anymore.

But he did.

He took every downward thrust, and he met her with an upward plunge. Harder, faster, until her forehead wrinkled and her cheeks flushed and her lips parted. Her fingers dug into his shoulders and she arched her neck.

He caught her fierce cry with his mouth and gathered her close as she shook, her climax rolling over her, consuming her. Her body milked his hard length and the fierce spasms proved too much. He exploded, his arms locked around her as he held himself deep inside and her close to him, and rode the sweet tide of ecstasy.

It was several minutes later before Austin finally found his voice. "That was incredible," he murmured, pressing a kiss against her soft hair.

"Mmm. I don't think I ever want to move from here."

The minute she said the words, his ears tuned to the steady *bam, bam, bam* coming from the front door.

"Are you expecting anyone tonight?"

She leaned back and reality seemed to register. She closed her eyes. "It's Uncle Spur. I locked the door in case he came back early. I was hoping he would make an evening of it—there're an awful lot of women to look over at senior's night at the bowling alley— but something must have happened. At least he had the good sense to hold off until we finished."

As Austin helped Maddie with her clothes, he recalled her proposition: *"Just once I want to know what it would feel like. You and me and sex. Some down and dirty, hot and heavy sex."*

Well, they'd had their *once,* and now it was over.

That's what Austin kept telling himself as he pulled on his own clothes, then opened the door to a cranky Uncle Spur. He didn't bother with small talk. He couldn't. He was still wound too tight, still overwhelmed by what had just happened. He said a quick good-night, walked out to his truck and headed home.

On the way, he rolled the windows down and drew a deep breath of fresh air to push the scent of her from his nostrils.

Now he could stop fantasizing about what she would taste like, smell like, look like, feel like lost in the throes of an orgasm. He knew, and so he could stop wondering and get back to the business of finding himself a forever kind of woman.

He'd stopped wondering, all right. But he couldn't seem to stop *remembering.* The knowledge followed him home, crawled into bed with him and distracted him even more than his fantasies.

So much for working her out of his system.

"I KNOW IT SOUNDS a little unconventional since we're looking for sexy, but trust me on this," Duane told Madeline when he phoned her early the next morning. "It comes from a very reliable source."

Madeline took a big gulp of her diet cola, prayed for the caffeine to send her a wake-up jolt after a restless night spent thinking about Austin and wanting more. More of his kisses and his touches. Once hadn't been nearly enough.

The notion might have made her a little nervous except for the fact that this was Austin. The man she'd thought about, fantasized about, wanted since the moment she'd written that love letter to him so long ago.

Not that this had anything to do with love. She'd been infatuated then and she was infatuated now. And it only stood to reason that it would take more than one quick, albeit spectacular, encounter on the sofa to sate years of lust.

She would need at least one more round to do that.

"Are you there?" Duane asked, drawing her back to the matter at hand.

"I'm here." She stared at the jar she'd pulled from the brown-paper-wrapped box Duane had overnighted her. "Reliable source, huh?"

"Luv4sale.com."

"Move over *Science Digest*."

"It's one of the top ten Internet sites for sexual

enhancement products. This is straight from their edible line of body paints. It jumped out at me because it isn't one of the usual flavors—strawberry, cherry, chocolate, that sort of thing. It's not one of their top sellers, and it's no wonder. I tried it and it leaves an awful aftertaste. Probably the adhesive base they use to make it stick to the body. Anyhow, I know you—you'll take the initial concept, work your magic and come up with something fabulous.''

"Maybe.''

"Hey, pumpkin pie gets my juices flowing.''

"You're ruled by your stomach.''

"Isn't every man?''

She remembered Austin's sweet-potato comments. Candied sweet potatoes contained sugar and cinnamon and nutmeg, and therefore had a similar flavor to pumpkin pie. "It *is* different, and that's what we need.''

"You said it. Now do it so we can land that promotion and move up in the world. No one should have to work in such poor conditions.''

"My lab is state-of-the-art. It has everything.''

"It doesn't have a hot plate. This going back and forth to heat up my snacks and lunch is killing me.''

"It's not supposed to have a hot plate. It's a sterile laboratory.''

Unlike the kitchen, where she sat with its gingham curtains and view of the sunporch filled with plants and a drooling Twinkles. Forget sterile. And professional.

Even so, she sort of liked it.

The minute the notion struck, she forced it aside. It was a far cry from her lab, which she missed with a passion.

"Just go over the test results I sent you from yesterday and put them in quantitative order."

"Yes, boss," he muttered before he hung up the phone. "I live to serve."

Madeline opened the jar, dipped her finger inside and sampled a taste. Ugh. The Internet site definitely needed a heads-up in product development.

But the concept *was* good. Different. Just what Madeline needed if she wanted to secure her position as chief of research and development and tempt Austin into another round of hot lovemaking tonight.

Not that she had to tempt him. After last night, she felt sure he would be more than ready to pick up where they'd left off. She shoved the jar back into the box and walked to the cupboard. A few minutes later, she'd made a list of ingredients to buy for tonight's test. She made a quick trek up the stairs and looked in on Uncle Spur, who snored loudly, still sound asleep after his evening at the bowling alley. She changed clothes and dabbed on a little makeup.

Downstairs, she checked on Twinkles who sat, tongue lolling and tail wagging, in front of the portable TV set tuned to *Regis and Kelly*. She grabbed the watering pitcher and went down the row of plants. A few soil pellets and a George Strait CD later, she finished with her chores and returned to the kitchen for her list.

She swatted at the dog hair that sprinkled her blue T-shirt—daily vacuuming and she still couldn't get it all—before grabbing her purse and heading off to the Piggly Wiggly.

She smiled as she slid behind the wheel. Last night Austin had finally seen for himself that she was no longer the shy, unattractive, geeky girl she'd been way back when. She was a sexy, attractive, take-charge woman.

And she still wanted him.

At least once more before she packed up her make-shift lab and headed back to the big city and the rest of her life, she would have him.

"JUST CALM DOWN, sweetheart," Austin ground out as he gripped the two pieces of barbed wire and tried to work them apart and over the cow's head.

The animal bellowed loud and deep, the sound making his already aching head hurt even more than the hot noonday sun was.

"Hollering isn't going to do you a bit of good," he muttered to the animal. "It'll be over—" he pulled and tugged "—in just a few seconds." More pulling and tugging and the animal finally scrambled free. One frantic hoof punched Austin in the stomach before he could lean out of the way. The air bolted from his lungs and pain ripped through him.

"Women," a familiar voice drawled behind him. "Can't live without them, but nobody in his right mind would ever want to live with them. That's for damned sure."

Pain gripped his body for a few breathless seconds before subsiding. He gasped for air and glanced up at the man who sat astride one of Austin's favorite chestnut mares.

While Austin and his youngest brother Dallas both had the same dark hair as their mother, Houston was the spitting image of their father.

Bick Jericho had been tall, tanned and blond, with whiskey-colored eyes and a killer smile, before he'd gotten himself saddled with a wife and the first of three unwanted children.

But in between the fighting and the drinking, things hadn't been so bad. There'd been those few precious sober moments when Bick Jericho would pick up his oldest son and plant him on his shoulders and walk around. Austin had felt so tall and proud and loved. Even if only for a few moments.

Houston's birth had added more pressure. Bick, who'd never been one for responsibility, had felt even more trapped. The arguments had turned into a daily occurrence and the drinking spells had come more often, lasting longer each time.

Dallas had come along a short time later and strained not only the marriage, but their mother's health. She'd been a diabetic and having a third child had been too much for her. Her kidneys had been pushed to the breaking point and, after seventeen months of dialysis, she'd died.

Austin had been only five at the time, but he could still remember the day they'd buried her. He'd stood there, flanked by his two younger brothers—Houston barely three and Dallas only a year and a half—and watched the casket disappear into the ground. He hadn't cried. He'd been afraid of scaring his two younger brothers who were holding so tightly to his hands. But he'd wanted to.

He'd wanted to cry because, despite that she'd been a far from perfect mother, he'd still loved her. Just as he'd loved his father.

Frequent drinking spells turned into a way of life. His dad had gone straight home, climbed into a bottle and never climbed back out.

Austin hadn't just lost his mother that awful day. He'd lost both parents—however imperfect—and the memory had haunted him every day thereafter.

For his brothers it had been different. They'd been so young that neither remembered very much about their life before. Or their mother. Or the semidecent man their father had been during his sober moments.

Austin eyed his younger brother. "It's been four days since the happy occasion. I would have figured you long gone by now."

"I don't have to be in Vegas for another two weeks. I figured I would stick around for Miss Marshalyn's party. No need in making another trip back. Thought I'd give you a hand out here in the meantime." He grinned. "You sure as hell look like you could use it. Never thought I'd see the day when a woman brought my oldest brother to his knees."

"You're a real comedian." Austin fingered his bruised middle and determined he'd suffered no broken ribs, then hauled himself to his feet.

"I'm even better with cows than I am at telling jokes, so this is definitely your lucky day."

Austin yanked off his gloves and shoved them into his hip pocket. "If that were the case, you'd be offering to stick around permanently by taking the hundred acres next door."

Houston shook his head. "I've got a bull with my name on it waiting at the PBR finals. Not to mention a dozen or so women ready to scream my name in the heat of the moment and walk away the morning after."

"Sounds awful lonely to me."

"I like things the way they are just fine. Besides, I'm not half as attached to the land as you are. Now if she'd offered the house, that would be another story."

"Really?"

He shrugged. "Maybe. Maybe not. But it's no never mind because she didn't. So can you use the help or not?"

Austin grinned. "I've got three fences down on the far west corner, and a nail gun with your name on it." His expression grew serious. "I've said it before and I'll say it again, you're welcome to stay out at my place."

"And be that much closer to Miss Marshalyn?" Houston shook his head. "That woman's driving me nuts, not to mention ruining my social life. She actually announced to her choir group that I came back to town to find a wife. Since then I've had at least a half dozen women knocking on my door over at the inn. Not the walk-away kind of women, either. These are the ones determined to stick around the morning after, and every day from then on. I've even got one in particular following me around town.''

"So now the truth comes out. You aren't so interested in helping out as you are in hiding out.''

Houston gave him a level stare. "Actually, I'm interested in both. You've got a pretty nice setup here. I'm real proud of you, bro.''

"Thanks.'' He glanced around before meeting Houston's gaze again. "And about Miss Marshalyn. Cut her some slack. She's just worried about you.''

"I'm a grown man now.''

"You're a *single* grown man.''

He grinned. "And I'm staying that way.'' He gathered the reins and steered the horse around. "I'll head back in, pick up the supplies from the barn and get started on the fence.''

Austin nodded and watched his brother ride off before he limped over to his own horse and retrieved the liniment from his saddlebags. Gathering his strength, he turned toward the wounded cow. She'd quieted down, easing the pounding in his temples.

He stepped toward her, his approach as easy as his voice. "Look, I haven't had more than an hour's sleep. I'm tired and hurting and I've had just about enough.'' Of the cow, that is.

He hadn't had nearly enough of sexy-as-hell Maddie Hale, which was the cause of his headache and his lack of sleep. He was the king of one-night stands, as in *one* night. That night was now over, but damned if he didn't want another.

A realization that confused the hell out of him. One night had always been just fine with him.

But now…he wanted more, and he wasn't sure what to do about it.

He knew what he *wasn't* going to do about it.

He wasn't having sex with her again. He'd made a lot of mistakes in his life, but he had the gut feeling that that would be his biggest. Better to curb his appetite before he really developed a taste for her, because, like it or not, Maddie was strictly temporary with her big-city job and her big-city life and her big-city ideas.

He may have seen glimpses of the shy, uncertain girl he'd once known, but she'd definitely changed. She wasn't the marrying kind.

Not anymore.

# 9

MADELINE HAD SEEN many things in her lifetime. After all, she was a worldly woman who lived in a major metropolis. Not much could shock her.

Except walking into her hometown Piggly Wiggly—the size of most convenience stores in Dallas—and smelling the scent of cinnamon rolls baking in a nearby oven.

An oven?

"Things just haven't been the same since they expanded with a bakery," Camille Skeeter told her. The old woman had been picking up some lemons—Skeeter's had many things but fresh produce wasn't part of the inventory—when she'd spotted Madeline and waved her over. "But the folks in town were desperate." A cough punctuated the sentence and she shook her head. "I hope this lemon tea works for my danged old croup. I've got an appointment with the doctor first thing Monday, but I'd hate to spend the rest of the week in misery. Ben's got a dinner over at the new nursing home on Friday night and I was hoping to go with him." Another cough and she cleared her throat.

Madeline followed the smell of cinnamon to a small counter at the rear of the store. Stacks of clear plastic containers holding freshly baked cinnamon rolls covered the top. Beyond stood a large silver oven and a preparation table. A man worked diligently to box more rolls. "They're actually *baking* back there."

"More like reheating. We haven't had any home-made baked goods in this town since your folks closed up shop and moved to the Coast. Except for Marshalyn. But since her eyesight's fading, she hasn't had much business. She's got folks running scared." At Madeline's questioning glance, Camille added, "For Norman Crater's retirement party over at the Elks Lodge, his wife ordered a double-chocolate-fudge layer cake with dark fudge filling."

Madeline's stomach grumbled at the thought and Camille smiled.

"Exactly. There isn't a person alive can resist all that chocolate. But Marshalyn mixed up her baking chocolate with her stress relief—the chocolate chewable kind that works in twenty-four hours—and the Elks had to have one of their bathrooms completely redone after that. Folks started to make do with the Piggly Wiggly stuff after that, but they still complained and so the manager, that nice Mr. Connally, responded to customer demand. He put in an oven and started heating up frozen stuff. The rolls are good for about the first ten minutes. Then they cool and you can taste the staleness."

Despite Camille's warning about the boxed goodies, Madeline was lured by the smell. After she said good-bye to the woman and promised to drop by some new lotion samples, she bought a dozen. She tore off a bite as soon as she walked out of the store.

Yep, Camille had been right.

No melting in your mouth. No watering taste buds. No craving for more. That's what her daddy's home-made chocolate éclairs, along with the rest of his offerings, had done for the town of Cadillac.

She wasn't sure if it was the strange sense of loneliness that stole through her or her craving for a home-made blueberry muffin, or maybe a little of both. But instead of heading back to her car, she walked the half block to her parents' old shop.

Most of the windows had been boarded up from the inside. A For Sale sign hung on the front door, the contact a local real-estate investment company who'd bought the place from her parents because of its prime commercial location. There'd been rumors of a diner opening up, but the buyer hadn't been able to get a loan approved and so the place still stood, waiting for a new owner, the ovens cold and silent inside.

It was so unlike the place she remembered, filled with lots of noise and sweet smells and warmth. Her favorite place where she'd learned her father's secret recipe for everything from cream puffs to blueberry muffins.

She could remember those Saturday nights when she and Sharon would strap on aprons and help her father prepare for the Sunday-morning rush. They would mix up dough, laugh and bake and sample goodies late into the night. It hadn't been the typical Saturday night, but it had always been fun. A wave of nostalgia rolled through her and she had the sudden urge to pull the For Sale sign from the window.

Crazy.

Madeline wouldn't be caught dead purchasing the run-down bakeshop. She didn't go near a kitchen any-more—not for baking purposes anyhow—much less a jelly doughnut or an apple fritter or a blueberry muffin.

Sure, she indulged with the occasional Oreo, but it was a purely creative necessity. A new craving she'd developed after she'd left her old life behind. But the craving didn't control her. She controlled it. When she wasn't in the lab, she walked the straight and narrow road of self-control, far removed from the frumpy, muffin-baking, overweight girl who'd once considered continuing the family business.

She needed noise and buildings and *life*.

Already she was feeling nervous and anxious and caged in. The sudden trembling in her hands proved as much.

"Hey, there, Maddie!" a woman's familiar voice called to her from across the street and drew her attention from the haunting images.

Madeline turned to see Eden Hallsey Weston stand-ing in front of the Pink Cadillac, the bar and grill situated directly across from her parents' shop.

At one time, the petite blonde had been quite the wild child. But since marrying Brady Weston, ex-captain of the football team and the All-American cowboy who headed his family's boot-making busi-ness, she'd traded her bad-girl ways for domestic bliss. Instead of short shorts and a tank top, she wore white capri pants and a baseball jersey that read Go Weston Wranglers! She had her arms overloaded with a pair of matching blond-haired, blue-eyed toddler boys.

Adjusting the boys in her arms, she glanced both ways before crossing the street and approaching Madeline.

"I saw you at Cheryl Louise's wedding, but I didn't really get a chance to catch up. How have you been doing? You look so good!"

"Thanks. So do you." Despite her obvious load, she was as pretty as ever. But even more than pretty, Eden looked happy.

The woman beamed. "It's hectic with these two underfoot, but I wouldn't trade it for anything. Brady and I like the whole parent thing so much we're working on number three." She shook her head. "Can you believe it? *Me?* A wife and a mother?"

"I bet you're great at both."

"I don't know about that, but I love being both. Go figure. So what about you? You have anybody special right now?"

The question stirred an image of Austin Jericho with his shirt pushed up and his fingers twined in her hair and his dark eyes glittering down at her while she suckled him.

"I'm too busy for a serious relationship."

"That's right," Eden said. "You're a big-time scientist with that cosmetics company. That must be very exciting."

Not half as exciting as the image of Austin.

She forced the notion aside and smiled. "It's more work than excitement, but I like it."

"I know what you mean. Running the bar was always that way for me until Brady." She glanced at her watch. "Speaking of which, Brady's company's softball team is playing the Kerrville Kangaroos in fifteen minutes and I promised to pick up sandwiches. I hired this really great cook and he makes the best brisket po'boys." At Madeline's questioning expression, she added, "With Brady and the kids, I had to cut back my hours at the bar. I only go in two days a week to oversee the books and the inventory. I've got a manager who runs things now."

"A manager?"

She nodded. "She's a godsend. Gotta run, but it was good seeing you. Good luck with your job!"

"Good luck with the whole mom and wife thing." Madeline watched Eden cross the street and disappear into the Pink Cadillac, and did her best to ignore the strange sense of longing that suddenly filled her.

Longing?

Because Eden was a mom and a wife?

Actually, the longing was more because Eden was a mom and wife and she seemed so happy about it. She'd even given up much of what she'd spent years working to build.

Not Madeline. She had plans. Goals. She wanted to go somewhere in her life, to move all the way to the top of V.A.M.P.'s research and development, and she was this close.

She gave the shop one last glance before starting

back up the street. She'd wasted too much time with silly reminiscing. She was all about getting things done now. In store for the evening was another test. And another round of sex so that she could work Austin completely out of her system.

She prayed they were both a success.

"ARE YOU READY?" Austin ducked his head in the doorway of Miss Marshalyn's house late Tuesday afternoon, fully expecting to see her wearing one of her nice polyester pantsuits and matching accessories. Her "going out" clothes. Instead, she wore a purple housedress and matching Keds. The sleeves were rolled up and she was submerged up to her elbows in a sink full of suds.

"Why aren't you ready for choir practice?"

"I'm not going." She pulled her hands free and grabbed a dish towel.

"But you never miss practice."

"I am today. I'm tired. I was out late bowling last night." She folded the used towel and set it back on the counter. "You'll never guess who was there."

"Spur Tucker."

"Spur Tucker, of all people," she went on as if she hadn't heard him. "He was going around to all the women, eating their nachos and taking bites of their frito pies. It was positively scandalous."

"Did you give him a bite of your pie?" His eyes twinkled.

"I was eating a hot dog, and the only thing I gave him was a piece of my mind."

Austin glanced at his watch. "So what about choir practice? Time's wasting."

"I already told you, I'm not going," she said again. "I hate choir."

"You love to sing."

"I hate the old biddies I sing with."

"They're your best friends."

"Some friends." She snorted. "I told them all last night I was bringing my special recipe fudge pie today." She indicated the dessert sitting on her kitchen table. A strange aroma filled the air. "I had just pulled it from the oven when Arsell Jenkins called and said she was bringing her coconut cake. She said the girls took a vote last night after I left and I'm out of the dessert rotation. They said that I can't bake to save my life anymore."

"What does baking have to do with choir? You love to sing." Not to mention, singing was safe for someone with poor eyesight. No walking involved. Just standing in the same spot, clapping and tapping every now and then.

"I can't go to choir practice without bringing something."

"So buy something."

She pinned him with a stare. "Are you implying that they're right?"

"No one bakes like you." He gave the pie and its funny smell a wide birth as he rounded the table. "It's not your baking." He came up to her, took her hand and said the one thing they both already knew. "It's your eyesight, sugar."

"My eyesight is perfectly fine," she huffed, snatching her hand away. She sank down at the kitchen table and Austin had no choice but to take the seat she motioned him into.

The smell grew stronger and his eyes started to water.

"Do you know what else Arsell said? She said that the girls think I have Old Timer's, and that my baking mistakes were because I'm starting to lose it upstairs." She tapped her temple. "Can you imagine? Me? With Old Timer's? Why, I can recite every scripture Pastor Standley has ever read at Wednesday night Bible study. I do not get mixed up. I simply made one itsy-bitsy mistake with Cheryl Louise's groom's cake. Sugar and salt. Both white. It was just an honest mistake. People make them all the time."

"If it's just a mistake, chances are it won't happen again. You shouldn't go making any rash decisions about quitting choir based on one honest mistake."

"True, but Arsell and the others think I have Old Timer's, and if I happen to make another mistake, then they'll make a big deal. I refuse to have the entire town wagging their collective tongue. I'd rather sing at home. At least then maybe they'll feel bad."

He folded his arms and eyed her. "Or you could talk to Dr. Bartlett about the eye surgery he mentioned during your last appointment."

"My sight is just fine for a woman my age," she insisted. "Speaking of which, I haven't seen you out and about with anyone lately. You're not dating, are you?"

"I'm working on it."

"My going-away party is the weekend after next. You'd better work a little harder. Unless you've changed your mind. In that case, I could give that real estate man a call and put this old place up for sale to some anonymous stranger who's never even set foot here and will no doubt bulldoze everything. Maybe even put up a few condos."

"We're out in the middle of nowhere. Nobody puts up condos in Nowhere, Texas."

"Maybe they'll open up one of those dude ranches and have all sorts of people coming and going, and they'll still have to bulldoze because they'll want modern lodging and probably a spa and a golf course and tennis courts—"

"Nobody's bulldozing anything." He frowned and turned. "I've got a woman in mind."

"Who?"

"If you're not going to choir, then I'll get back to work." He pushed to his feet.

"Who?" She followed him out onto the front porch. "Come on. Say something."

"If I were you, I wouldn't let a bunch of gossips keep me from doing something I enjoy. Go to choir practice anyway. Show those old women that they can't keep a good woman down."

"That's not what I wanted you to say. Tell me her name."

"Have a nice day, Miss Marshalyn." He tipped his hat and stepped off the front porch, his boots eating up dust as fast as his legs could carry him before he had to admit the truth—that he still hadn't decided on any one suitable woman in particular.

Now if they were talking a hot, brazen, totally unsuitable woman…well, he'd found her, all right.

Talk about bad luck.

FORGET BAD. His luck was plumb rotten.

Austin came to that conclusion when Madeline met him at the door wearing a thin white silk blouse tucked into a tight black skirt. She hadn't bothered to wear a bra and her nipples made mouthwatering points beneath the flimsy material. Her breasts trembled with every breath she took.

It took everything he had not to pull her into his arms, peel the shirt from her and return the attention she'd lavished on his own nipples the night before.

He focused on walking to the sofa and sitting down in his usual spot. She came around him and the blindfold slid into place. Next came the scarf at his wrists.

"We didn't do this last night."

"Because I needed your arms free to try out the samples on your skin. Tonight we're isolating your sense of taste. So no touching." She tied the ends into place and checked her work. "Unless you start to feel dizzy. If so, tell me and I'll see what I can do."

A few moments later, the couch dipped just to his left.

Several moments passed where Austin heard nothing save the frantic beat of his heart as he waited. And waited.

"What are you doing?"

"Getting ready," she said, her voice soft and sweet and slightly amused. "Be patient."

"I've got work to do—"

"Now," she breathed. "I'm definitely ready."

He should have known by the way she said the words that something was up—besides his dick, that is. But he was so fixated on getting started and getting out of there that nothing else registered.

"Let's go," he told her, his fingers clasped together. "Let's get it over with."

"Okay. I'm going to hold the first sample up. Take a lick and tell me what you taste in three descriptive words."

His lips parted and his tongue darted out and he lapped a dollop of a creamy, puddinglike substance. The sweet taste of raspberries with an underlying hint of salty skin exploded in his mouth and he quickly realized that she wasn't holding the sample with a spoon. She'd dipped her finger into the mixture and held it out to him.

He swallowed and his head snapped back. "What the hell are you doing?" he sputtered.

"Administering the sample."

"With your finger."

"So what?"

"So shouldn't you use a spoon, or fork or...*something?* Anything but your finger?"

"I could just scoop it into my palm if you'd like."

"It's not about what I like. It's about the fact that this is a taste test. Taste as in eat. Most people eat with a damned spoon or something."

"I need to know how the subtle flavor of skin mingles with the actual sample, and how palatable the combination is. That's why you have to taste the lotion as it was meant to be used—slathered onto a warm body. My warm body."

The moment she said the words, he envisioned her peeling off her shirt and smoothing the sample over her ripe nipples and letting him take a nice long lick.

His jeans strained over his massive erection and he shifted for a more comfortable position.

"Are you okay?" Her whisper raised the hair on the back of his neck. She sounded so breathless, so sexy, so...*warm*.

He tried to shake away the sudden image of wild and wicked Madeline stretched out on the couch, naked except for a thin sheen of lotion.

"I didn't mean to surprise you," she went on. "I figured it would be obvious that we need to do it this way."

"Well, yeah," he said, his voice tight and strained. It also made the situation much harder than he'd anticipated. *Harder* being the key word.

*Descriptive words*, he told himself. *Just describe the damned thing and get this over with.*

But he couldn't. With all the talk, he'd lost the full impact of the taste and now he needed another.

"Let me try it again." He opened his mouth. He meant to lick. At least that's what he told himself. But instead, his damned mouth seemed to have its own agenda, and it wanted a taste. A real taste.

His lips closed around the tip of her finger. He suckled, drawing a gasp from her before he drew the tip deeper into the warm heat of his mouth. He sucked and laved her skin, savoring the taste of her mingled with the raspberries. A potent combination.

"Potent," he murmured when he finally pulled back and drank in a deep breath. "Powerful."

"And?" She sounded breathless, as if the contact had affected her the way it had affected him.

"Sweet."

"That's good. Now we'll move on to number two."

He expected a finger. Instead, she'd slathered the sample onto the inside of her wrist, which she touched to his lips.

He tasted sweet vanilla and sugar, like frosting, and he couldn't resist. He lapped at the creamy substance until he reached bare skin. He licked the last bit of sweetness and pressed his lips against her frantic pulse for a long moment.

"I…" she started, seeming at a loss for words. Almost as if bold and brazen Madeline had suddenly lost her nerve.

The realization eased his own anxiety and turned it to something darker and more determined.

"Cupcakes," he breathed as he pulled away. "You taste like cupcakes. Sweet and moist and…" He lapped one final time at the tender inside of her wrist and made her catch her breath. "Sticky," he finished.

"I…" she began again, then cleared her throat. "I mean, good. That was really good. Let's move on to number three. Try this one," she said.

His tongue darted out and touched soft, fragrant skin

smoothed with sweet lotion that tasted like…chocolate. It didn't matter that Austin had always been partial to everything from vanilla ice-cream cones to Twinkies rather than Ding Dongs. Suddenly it was all about the mouthwatering flavor coating his tongue.

And what was one more little taste?

He licked and nibbled, his lips pressed to the delicate skin as he devoured the sample. Her breath caught and her free hand touched the back of his neck as if to brace herself. Or hold him close.

Either way, her fingers scorched him and made him even more ravenous. He ate at her until he sucked bare, salty skin that tantalized his taste buds even more than the delicious chocolate.

"Rich," he breathed as his lips worked an inch up the tender inside of her upper arm. He felt the fullness of her breast against his cheek and it was all he could do not to turn and suckle her right through her blouse. But he wasn't that far gone.

Not yet.

"Sweet," he added, moving another inch higher. "Sinful."

"No more," she said, her voice slightly pleading.

"Isn't this what you wanted?" He kissed her skin.

"I mean the sample." Her words pushed past the fog of desire gripping his senses. "There's no more. We should move on to the next one."

He pulled away, his heart pounding as he waited for what would come next. A dozen possibilities flashed in his mind before long, silky fingers finally threaded through his hair and turned his head sideways before guiding his lips down.

More luscious skin smoothed with the flavor of candied apples mesmerized his taste buds and he reacted like a starving man. He licked and nibbled until a frantic thud pulsed against his mouth and he realized his location.

Her neck.

*Whoa, buddy. This is bad. Real bad.*

But even as the warning echoed through his head, he lifted his bound hands and touched her neck with his fingertips, desperate for more than just a taste. He needed to feel her, to soak up her softness and consume it the way he was consuming the cream smoothed over her delicious skin.

Trailing his fingertips down, he felt his way to the deep vee of her cleavage. He lingered at the warm skin there for a moment as he nibbled. Then he touched one silk-covered nipple.

He circled the nub, feeling it ripen even more beneath his touch. He needed to taste her, to feel the hard tip against his lips and suck her into the wet heat of his mouth.

Despite his bound hands, he made quick work of the buttons, feeling his way from one to the next until he shoved the material aside. He kissed a path to her nipple and was about to close his mouth over her when she pushed him away.

"Wait." She moved, scooting a few inches away. "We've got another sample."

But he wasn't of a mind to wait. Snagging the edge

of the tie around his wrist, he pulled and the material loosened. He slid his hands free. Then he reached for the blindfold, pulling the silk down just in time to see her touch a dollop of burnt orange cream to her rosy-red nipple.

"Aw, hell," he groaned. At the sound of his voice, her head snapped up and her hand froze.

"You're supposed to keep your senses isolated." Her words drew his attention to her face. To the flush of her cheeks and the desire burning in her eyes and the wet fullness of her lush mouth. Her tongue swiped across her bottom lip and his insides hollowed out.

He tried to find his voice, but he couldn't. He hadn't had the chance to really *look* last night, and Christ, she looked beautiful. Wanton. Wild.

"Go ahead," she said, as if she mistook his silence for confusion. "Take a taste."

Oddly enough, it wasn't the bold, brazen way she said the words that made him grow even harder. It was the jolt of pure lust that shot through him, as if he hadn't just had one of the best climaxes of his life not more than twenty-four hours ago. That, and something else. A need more fierce than anything he'd ever felt before.

He reached out, touched his fingertip to her nipple. The bud hardened even more, pressing and tightening, reaching out. He drew in a shaky breath and brought the dab of cream on his finger to his own lips. The warm flavor of pumpkin combined with cinnamon and sugar set his mouth watering and hunger gnawed at his insides.

"That's not what I meant," she told him.

"I know," he told her. He kissed her roughly, his fingers threading through her hair as he held her for the onslaught of his lips and tongue.

Then he buttoned her blouse, stood and walked away before he stopped thinking with his head and gave in to his damned body again.

She was a one-night stand, as in one, as in temporary, and as much as he wanted to forget that fact, he couldn't.

He wouldn't.

Not with his land, and his heart, hanging in the balance.

THE DOOR SLAMMED SHUT behind Austin and he drank in the night air, eager to calm his pounding heart.

"Damn, but that was close," he muttered.

"You ain't just whistling Dixie." The crackly voice came from Austin's left. He glanced to the side to see the old man braced against the porch rail. "You and Maddie been watching that *Exorcist* marathon that's on cable tonight?"

"What?"

"'Cause the way you came barreling outa there, a fella would think the devil himself was right on your heels."

"More like a she-devil." As in red-hot and on fire, and the *last* type of woman Austin needed in his life right now.

"I think I need to sit down." Uncle Spur stumbled toward the porch swing.

"It's not your heart, is it?"

"My stomach."

Austin frowned. "I gave your stomach a start?"

"Marshalyn did that. You just scared the bejeesus out of me."

"I don't think I'm following you."

"You like pie, boy?"

"I'm from Texas, aren't I?"

"Well, so do I. That is, until I just tasted Marshalyn Simmons's famous fudge pie. See, I thought I'd mosey on over to the ladies' choir practice at the church and she was there with this good-looking dish. Said it was her prize-winning recipe and I believed her. Women," he shook his head. "You think they would just admit their shortcomings."

"You ate a slice of that pie?"

"Damn straight I did. It was okay going down, but then it had this funny little aftertaste. Come to find out, she mistook a bottle of cod-liver oil for her vanilla. I tell you, it was god-awful, and I ain't a religious man. I told her as much and you know what she had the nerve to tell me? That I was an insensitive old coot and she deserved an apology. When I said she should be the one apologizing for upsetting my digestive system, she busted out crying and locked herself in the ladies' room."

"You really said that?"

"'Course I said it. I always speak the truth. Insensitive," he muttered. "Why, I should be so lucky. As it is, I swear I dropped ten pounds before I managed to leave the church's rec building. If that ain't sensitive, at least in the stomach area, I don't know what is. Speaking of which—'' he bolted to his feet ''—I think I'd better get inside before the weight starts coming off again.

"An apology, of all things," he grumbled as he reached for the screen door. "If she's expecting one from me she'll be waiting till the cows come home 'cause I ain't done a cotton-pickin' thing. She should be the one calling and begging my forgiveness."

"MARSHALYN WON'T TAKE any of my phone calls," Uncle Spur announced three days later as he eyed Madeline over a bowl of Cheerios.

"You told her she was a rotten cook." Madeline took a long drink of her diet cola and ate a bite of whole-wheat toast.

"She is."

"But you didn't have to say it."

"I call 'em like I see 'em, is all. I'm an honest man. Ain't women always yackin' about how they want an honest man?"

"Honest as in *'Honey, I'm going to the store,'* and that's where you actually go. Not honest as in *'Yes, dear, your butt looks monumental in those orange capri pants.'*"

He glanced under the table. "You ain't wearin' orange capri pants—not that I know what capris are, but you ain't in pants—and your butt still looks—"

"That's exactly what I'm talking about, Uncle Spur." She waved her piece of toast at him. "I know my butt isn't the smallest in the state. Everyone else knows it, too. But there's no reason for you to constantly point it out.''

"If you know it, then what's the big deal if I point it out?''

"You can't spit tobacco near as well as your brothers, right?''

"What are you talking about?''

"About the fact that you used to chew and spit tobacco all the time. You spit on Janice's shoe that time when we were kids.''

"I don't spit anymore. It's bad for you.''

"True, but that's not why you gave it up. You gave it up because you came in third to your two brothers in the Waller County Spit-Off that time, right?''

His gaze narrowed. "And your point is?''

"You don't spit because you don't want to be reminded that you're third-rate.'' At his sharp look, she added, "Not that third is anything to be ashamed of. There were over fifty men in that competition and you put forty-seven of them to shame.''

"Damn straight I did.''

"That's an accomplishment, but at the same time, it wasn't your shining moment. Rather, one you would more than likely like to forget. But what if everybody kept reminding you of your shortcoming?''

"My brothers still rib me.''

"And it doesn't make you feel very good, does it? Even though it's old news, it still bothers you.''

"Ain't nothin' bothers old Spur, little gal,'' he muttered, but she could tell that he was thinking about what she'd said. "I don't mean to hurt nobody,'' he finally added. "Still, Marshalyn damn well knows she cain't cook anymore. I didn't tell her anything she didn't already know."

"True, but maybe she thinks the effort should count for something. Whether it was good or bad, she still spent all day slaving away near a hot oven. I'd say, good or bad, the fact that a woman would go to so much trouble should show what a good woman she is."

"She does have a good heart. A little loudmouthed at times, but nothing I cain't handle. I like to talk myself. She noticed it, too. She said she enjoyed talking to me at choir practice. Said she was surprised since she didn't think she liked me, but after jawing a little, she said I wasn't all that bad. Then I told her she was just the kind of woman I'd like to scoot up next to on a cold winter's night. Before I tasted her pie, that is."

"Does it really matter if she can cook?"

"Somebody has to."

"You do it. This is the new millenium. Men cook, too."

"I know that. Thought of it myself just last night, but it was too late. She's as mad as a misplaced hornet."

"I'd be mad myself."

"She wants an apology."

"I'd want one myself. A big one."

"An apology she ain't gettin'." At her pointed stare, he added, "How the heck am I supposed to apologize if she won't take my calls? It's too damned late, is what it is. I blew my chance.''

"Maybe." Madeline took a bite of her dry toast. Ugh. While she'd been content with the same old breakfast for the past several years, lately she'd been thinking that it just didn't taste all that great. Her senses were alive, especially after her failed seduction attempt with Austin a few nights ago. She craved some real gratification.

Something to ease the hunger deep inside her. Something sweet and loaded with fat and…comforting. Something bigger and a heck of a lot more mouthwatering than a measly Oreo cookie.

"And maybe not," she said as an idea struck.

"What do you mean?"

"Well, it's obviously going to take more from you than a simple 'I'm sorry.' Words are just words. Actions speak much louder if you want to get her back to thinking that you're not so bad."

"I still ain't following you."

"It's time for you to show her how you really feel about her. Reveal your romantic side."

"I ain't blowing some ungodly amount on some fancy schmancy flower bouquet from the Piggly Wiggly. That's a total waste of hard-earned money."

"It's not about buying her something, Uncle Spur. It's about effort. You need to make a grand effort to do something that's important to her. Cooking is obviously important to Miss Marshalyn or she wouldn't be so hurt that you insulted hers."

"True enough, but I'm still not following you."

"She likes sweets."

"So?"

"So make her something sweet."

"I ain't ever baked anything in my life. I can cook—stuff like Shit on the Shingles and Anything Goes Stew. But a pie?"

"Not a pie." She smiled, making a mental list of ingredients. "I think we can manage something a lot more impressive than a pie."

"We? As in you and me?"

"I wasn't talking about my two-butt cheeks." When he opened his mouth, she held up a hand. "Say one word, just *one,* and you'll be crawling into bed with Twinkles tonight."

"I wasn't going to say a word."

She grinned. "Maybe you're not such a lost cause, after all."

# 10

"THAT MAN IS A LOST CAUSE." Miss Marshalyn pulled the seat belt across her and snapped it into place. "Imagine him telling me that I can't cook."

"He told you that, huh?" Austin arched an eyebrow at her as he backed the truck out of her driveway and started toward town.

"His exact words were 'Damn, Marshalyn, but you couldn't cook your way out of a brown paper bag'." She shook her head. "Why, I've been cooking longer than most folks around here have been alive. It's not my cooking that's the problem. I can cook just fine. I just can't—" Her words stumbled to a halt and she gave him a sideways glance. "I can see just fine," she huffed.

"I'm not saying a word."

"It was an honest mistake. People make them all the time, not to mention that cod-liver-oil bottle looked exactly like my vanilla. Why, somebody ought to bring it to that vanilla company's attention. The whole situation screams lawsuit to me. Somebody could come along and be in desperate need of a good cleaning and they take the vanilla and get so stopped up that their head blows off."

"Or the opposite end." He grinned, but she didn't seem to share his amusement.

Guilt rushed across her face. "Spur needed a good cleaning out anyway. The man is full of crap. I'm the best cook this county has ever seen."

"I'm sure he knows that. I don't think he was talking about your reputation so much as last night, in particular. Hell, everybody has a bad day once in a while. Sometimes I can't rope a calf to save my life and my foreman is all too quick to point it out."

"Because he's ribbing you. Spur was not ribbing me, and if he was, it wasn't the least bit funny."

"I'm sure he didn't mean to hurt your feelings."

"My feelings are perfectly fine. I don't care what that old coot has to say. He isn't worth the cow dung I scraped off the bottom of my shoe this morning. He's stubborn and insensitive and ornery. Why, I've never met a more difficult man in my entire life."

"I seem to recall you huffing and puffing about someone else way back when."

"Jim wasn't that bad." The minute the words were out of her mouth, she shook her head. "Okay, so he was that bad, but I was married to the man. I had to put up with him. Spur Tucker means absolutely nothing to me and I don't have to listen to his lame apologies."

"Oh, he tried to apologize, did he?"

"He's called and left several messages on the answering machine."

"Why didn't you answer the phone?"

"Because I didn't want to. I have nothing to say to

him except good riddance. I hope he takes the next feed plane back to that decaying old house he calls a ranch because I'm not interested.''

"I hear his place is pretty respectable."

"He's seventy-three and never been married. I dread to even think what the inside of the place looks like.''

He wanted to point out that at the rate she was going it wouldn't matter because she wouldn't be able to see it with those eyes of hers, but he kept his mouth shut. As much as he wanted to toss her over his shoulder and cart her over to Austin Medical himself, he could only sit back and let her make her own decision. She was a grown woman and she was afraid. He didn't share her fear, but he understood it, and it was something she would have to deal with in her own time.

Or face the consequences.

"Whatever would I do out in the middle of nowhere? Why, I must have been crazy even to think that Spur Tucker might be worth his salt. I'm an exciting, vivacious woman. I've got too much to offer a man who gets excited over celebrity *Wheel of Fortune*. I need people. A social life. I bet the nearest church choir is two hours away.''

"I thought you quit choir."

"Nonsense. I need stimulation. Speaking of which, you'd better step on the gas and hurry it up before the line gets too long at the Toss-n-Tease. I've been suffering all week with this gray mess and I'm not about to go another minute. I thought Friday would *never* get here.''

"Were they all booked up during the week?"

"No."

"So why didn't you just go in sooner?"

"Friday is half-off all hair services."

"Miss Marshalyn, you've got Fort Knox stashed in your sofa cushions, not to mention I can't even imagine what your bank balance looks like. Money's not a problem for you. Of course, if it is, I'd be glad to write you a check this very minute for that one hundred acres."

"I just bet you would." She shook her head. "I've got plenty of money. Jim saw to that. Not to mention, my work at the library and my baking over the years have helped me accumulate a nice little nest egg." She cut him a sly glance. "And nobody's supposed to know about my sofa cushions."

"I hate to break it to you, but everybody knows."

"Why, that loudmouth Gwen—"

"Don't get all ruffled. Everybody knows and nobody cares. It's your money."

"Exactly. Which brings us back to half-off Friday. Why should I pay full price when I can save a nice little chunk? Besides, Friday is also food and friends day for the ladies' auxiliary who meet at the Toss-n-Tease." At his questioning glance, she added, "We kill three birds with one stone. In between the coloring and the perms, we're giving Camille Skeeter a get-well party. She's been feeling a little under the weather and so Dr. Blake is sending her to Austin for some routine testing. Merline says it's probably bronchitis. I think it's more allergies, myself. Margaret

Winchester swears it's a virus and I think Camille herself is leaning toward that. Whatever it is, a party is just what she needs. And a new haircut. That always perks me right up.''

"What's the third bird?"

"It's Bonnie Hanover's last week in Cadillac, so today will also be her going-away party."

"Food and friends, huh?"

"Don't worry. I didn't make anything. I've got two containers of store-bought dip in my purse."

"I'm sure Miss Hanover will be mighty grateful."

"Smart mouth," she snapped. "Forget grateful. Bonnie's just excited. She's moving to one of those retirement colonies outside of Austin. They have daily bingo *and* weekly casino bus trips *and* a monthly trip to the movies. Now there's a way to spend your glory years."

"I think plenty of sunshine and a beach full of hunky boy toys would be better for a vital, red-blooded female with a lot of years left under her belt."

Marshalyn frowned. "I get plenty of sunshine here and I can't stand those tight little swimming trunks some men wear. Why, they leave nothing to the imagination. A woman like me enjoys pondering a bit."

"Sounds like you're having second thoughts about moving to Miami."

"I'm having no such thing. It's just that Florida isn't all it's cracked up to be and I'm not afraid to say so, not to mention while I love my sister, she can be a bit loose at times. But then, she is younger."

"So don't go."

"And stay here so that you don't have to fulfill your promise? Not on your life, Austin Elijah Jericho. You're settling down if I have to spend twenty-four/seven until my dying breath sipping Bloody Marys poolside and watching a bunch of men shake their barely concealed assets right in my face. It's a small price to pay for my peace of mind."

"Yep, it sounds rough. Hey, I wonder what kind of swimming trunks Spur wears?"

"Do not try to change the subject."

"I'm not. We were talking about you and Tucker and last night."

"We were not. We were talking about your promise. Speaking of which, do you have anyone in mind for my party? It's only a week away, you know."

"Still a whole week?" The question earned him a glare and he grinned.

"Do you?"

"Do I what?"

"Have a date."

"No."

"Not even with sweet little Maddie Hale?" She smiled. "I heard from Della who heard from Gretchen that you've been going over to her place here lately."

"I'm helping her on one of her work projects, and she's not sweet."

"She was always such a nice girl. So thoughtful and sweet. She brought me chicken soup one time at the library when I had a terrible cold, not to mention she showed up every morning when I opened the doors with a nice, big, warm muffin in her hands."

"Trust me, she's changed. She's not the same woman." And he had the hard-on to prove it.

He flipped the air conditioner on high and adjusted the vents. The cool relief blasted him, but it wasn't enough to lower his already raging body temperature.

If only she had been the same Maddie, then maybe things between them could have been different.

"Her daddy made the best muffins in town," Marshalyn went on. "Well, almost. My strudel muffins did win at the county fair that one year for best breakfast cake. But Walter did have the market cornered when it came to blueberry and he taught Madeline every secret he knew. Why, toward the end of high school, I couldn't even tell a difference when she started bringing me her own muffins instead of his. You like muffins."

"Trust me, she's not making muffins anymore." She was making mischief with her sultry glances and her edible body lotions. "She hates to cook. In fact, she vowed off cooking when she left Cadillac."

"That doesn't sound like the Maddie I knew."

"That's what I keep telling you."

"Maybe you're wrong."

"And maybe I'll actually be able to find a parking place right in front of the beauty salon," he said as he steered the truck onto a very busy Main Street.

"Where's your faith, Austin?" Miss Marshalyn asked as they crept past the hair shop, the street lined on either side with cars.

"Back in Cheryl Louise's living room." Where

he'd had down and dirty sex with sweet Madeline Hale.

Austin pulled up in front of the shop. "Wait," he said when Miss Marshalyn reached for the door handle. He slid from the seat and rounded the hood.

"You've definitely turned into quite a gentleman." She beamed as he pulled open her door and reached for her hand to help her out.

It wasn't so much in the interest of manners as it was safety.

"Watch the curb."

"I've got it," she told him as she stepped down and teetered. "Stop fussing."

"Five seconds ago I was being a gentleman."

"Now you're being a fussy gentleman." She pulled her arm free and started in the general direction of the front door. Austin was right on her heels, his hand at her elbow helping to steer her past a flower pot that was dangerously close to the front door.

She managed just fine without him, most of the time. Except for last week when she'd tripped over her mop. Then again a few days ago when she'd stumbled and sat on the black lab puppy he'd given her this past Christmas. Both woman and animal were doing just fine, but Austin wasn't in any hurry to see the accidents escalate, particularly when concrete and moving vehicles were involved.

He intended to see her safely inside and into the nearest shampoo chair, which he did, pausing only to smile and greet the dozen or so women seated throughout the shop, all in various stages of primping.

"What a nice boy."

"What a polite boy."

"What a handsome boy."

"What a hottie."

He smiled at the last comment, pushed open the door and ran smack-dab into Spur Tucker.

"Hell's bells, boy," the old man grumbled as his head snapped up. "I think this is some sort of conspiracy."

"I didn't see you."

"Lately, you've got a bad habit of that." He straightened his shirt and peered beneath a red-checked napkin covering the contents of the small basket in his arms. "They look okay." His gaze zeroed in on Austin. "Otherwise, I'd have to whip your hind end for messing up my peace offering." He tugged at his starched collar and squared his shoulders. "Step aside, boy. I've got business inside."

"You sure you want to do this? You're outnumbered."

"A man's gotta do what a man's gotta do. Now step aside, boy, afore I change my mind."

"Good luck."

"Don't need it. I've got these on my side." He held up the basket and opened the door.

Austin inhaled, drinking in the aroma of blueberry muffins before the door rocked shut and the Toss-n-Tease swallowed up the old man. The scent stirred his memory, and for a split second, he was sitting in the library across from Maddie, munching one of her homemade muffins while she explained an algebra formula to him.

*Nah.*

The Piggly Wiggly must have branched out and added muffins to their cinnamon bun counter because Maddie—make that Madeline—didn't bake anymore.

That's what Austin told himself, until a flash of tanned skin and long blond hair caught the corner of his eye.

Austin turned in time to see Madeline disappear around the side of the Toss-n-Tease. She was standing on her tiptoes, peering in one of the side windows when he rounded the building.

The sight of her hit him hard and fast, stopping him in his tracks a few feet away. She wasn't all done up the way she had been every night for their test sessions. There wasn't a stitch of red spandex or a miniskirt in sight. Instead, she wore a pair of faded blue jean shorts and a white T-shirt imprinted with tiny yellow daisies. She'd pulled her hair up into a ponytail. Several long strands hung loose, sweeping down the side of her jaw. Her face was bare. No blush or lipstick or eyeliner. Nothing but a smudge of flour on one cheek and a smear of blueberry juice near her chin.

For all her protests when it came to cooking, she *had* made the muffins.

The truth hit him like a punch to the stomach and sucked the air from his lungs for five full heartbeats. She wasn't Madeline Hale, innocent turned she-devil, she was simply Maddie, the same Maddie who'd blushed and stammered and brought muffins to their tutoring sessions way back when, and he wanted her more than he'd ever wanted any woman before.

The feeling had nothing to do with the woman she'd become, and everything to do with the shy young woman she'd once been.

As much as she wanted to believe she'd changed, she was still the same inside. She'd merely been trying to hide who she really was. But he'd seen it in the way she blushed whenever he stared into her eyes, the way her lips trembled when he smiled at her, the way she lost her train of thought and repeated herself whenever he touched her, the way she'd marveled at the feel of his mouth between her legs.

He'd seen the signs, yet he'd been swayed by her looks and her words and constant insistence that she was nothing like the girl he'd once known. She was in denial, determined to keep running from her past, from her grief over Sharon.

From her fear that maybe, just maybe, that shy, young, innocent still lived and breathed deep inside her and the new life she'd built for herself away from Cadillac had just been a very vivid dream.

She was terrified of backsliding into her old insecurities and losing everything she'd worked so hard for—her job, her independence, her sense of self.

He knew what haunted her because it lived and breathed inside of him, as well.

The realization hit him as he stood there, staring at her as she smiled and peaked over the window ledge into the shop. It wasn't so much the way she looked on the outside, but the way she *looked*—the light that danced in her eyes, the smile that curved her luscious lips, the blush that pinked her bare cheeks and made her look more vibrant and alive than any makeup. That vitality came from the inside and it drew him more fiercely than a hot body or a pretty face.

She drew him on a deeper level because she knew his fear. She faced it herself.

Just like her, he was afraid of who he'd been, fearful of breaking his promise and discovering that deep down he was no better than the poor, troublemaking kid who'd raced his secondhand bike through Miss Marshalyn's prize-winning rosebushes. A kid who'd had no real home or values or even a conscience. Just a ready-made reputation and a pair of badass footsteps to follow in.

He hadn't cared about anyone or anything because he'd never had anyone or anything until Miss Marshalyn Simmons had fed him a meal and shown him that he did have someone who cared about him.

Eventually he'd made a home for himself and found a purpose and embraced responsibility, and he liked all three. But falling for a woman like all the others in his past would have proved the sheriff right—that people like Austin couldn't change. They were no-good troublemakers. It was in their blood, who they were, who they were meant to be.

*Born trouble.*

But he hadn't been born any such thing. He'd turned to trouble because he'd had little else in his life. Then. But now everything had changed. He'd changed. Being a Jericho didn't make him no good from the get-go. There was no predetermined destiny. There were choices. Chances. He'd taken his and made something of himself, and the fight was over. There was no reason to keep running, afraid to backslide, afraid to prove the sheriff and everybody else right.

He hadn't been seduced by Madeline the good-time she-devil. He'd fallen for the Maddie buried deep inside. The woman standing right in front of him, so close all he had to do was take two steps and make the first move this time.

He grinned and stepped forward.

# *11*

MADELINE PEERED over the window ledge and watched Uncle Spur hand his peace muffins to Miss Marshalyn.

The older woman didn't drop-kick the basket into the nearest trash can or stuff one of the megasize treats up Spur's nose, or any other orifice.

Definitely a good sign.

Good, but not great. Marshalyn wasn't smiling yet, despite the baked goodies and the fast movement of Uncle Spur's mouth—*uh-oh.*

Dread rushed through her as she watched the older woman's eyes narrow, her lips purse. He wouldn't... he couldn't...

Madeline shoved at the window, desperate to hear, but it was locked. She pressed her ear against the pane, but she heard little more than a murmur, the voices muffled by the glass and the whir of a nearby air conditioner.

"Don't say it," she murmured as she watched the older couple. "Please, don't say anything you're going to regret."

"Trust me, I'm not going to regret anything I'm about to say. Or do." The deep, husky voice slid into her ears a moment before she felt the tall, muscular male body step up behind her.

"What are you—" she whirled around "—doing?" A surprised gasp punctuated the sentence as she found herself pinned against the wall, Austin's arms braced on either side of her, his legs anchoring hers, his chest blocking out everything except the warm, enticing aroma of soap and wind and aroused male.

"What I should have done a long, long time ago." He leaned in, his lips brushing the shell of her ear as he inhaled. "You smell good." Another whiff and his chest expanded, brushing the tips of her nipples.

Desire knifed through her. Her breasts swelled, the peaks ripening, pushing out, desperate for another caress.

"I...it's the lotion that you smell." She'd spent the past three days evaluating the trial tests and putting together a final formula, which she'd promptly slathered on before she'd joined Uncle Spur in the kitchen to work on his apology to Marshalyn.

He inhaled again, his chest expanding, brushing her nipples in another agonizing caress, and her breath caught.

"Like warm sugar and blueberries," he murmured.

*Raspberry sorbet.* That's the flavor she'd put on that morning. The fact registered along with an inkling that something wasn't right. But then he moved his head and his tongue flicked out just to the right of her lips.

"You taste good, too," he murmured.

"It's the lotion. Raspberries flavored with vanilla."

"Sugar and blueberries." He reached up and rubbed

his thumb over the spot he'd just licked and she all but melted into a puddle at his feet. "You feel good, too."

"Lotion," she blurted, her chest heaving as she tried for a deep, calming breath. Her heart was beating much too fast and her hands were trembling because, for the first time, Austin was actually taking the initiative with her.

"Soft and sticky," he went on. He pulled back to gaze into her eyes. "And you look good. Your cheeks are flushed."

"It's part of the visual enhancement. The lotion gives me a rosy hue. We didn't test for that. It's a given."

"You look hot," he told her. "Aroused. Are you?"

*Yes!*

The response screamed in her head as she stared into his eyes and saw the dark heat that simmered just below the surface. A look she instantly recognized from the nights he'd been at the house with her. From all those years ago when she'd faced him that night at the football game.

He wanted her.

Not that the fact was late-breaking news. He'd wanted her then. And he'd wanted her since she'd rolled back into town and into his arms at Cherry Blossom Junction.

But he'd held back and she'd had to take the initiative.

Not this time.

It was as if something had changed between them.

As if the tide had shifted in her favor. As if Austin Jericho had surrendered to his lust and accepted it.

*Right.*

While she might have changed enough to seduce him into the sack at least once, she wasn't hot enough to keep him there. That fact had sunk in three nights ago as she'd watched his headlights disappear down the street, and then she'd done what any woman who'd just been rejected would do—she'd eaten an entire bag of Oreos.

Only this time it hadn't made her feel better. Instead, she'd felt sick and defeated, and all because of one pigheaded, aggravating, frustrating, sexy-as-sin man.

While she'd changed, she hadn't changed nearly enough. Not enough to drive him over the edge and get him to make the first move. She'd faced that fact on Tuesday night and to entertain anything different now would only lead to more heartache.

Not that her heart was involved, mind you. It was her pride. Her self-esteem. Her ego.

He'd shattered all three with his reluctance and she wasn't about to get her hopes up only to let him do it to her all over again.

He wasn't coming on to her and making the first move.

*He was coming on to her and making the first move.*

His lips played over hers, his tongue licking, teasing, begging her to open her mouth and she did. He plunged inside, his tongue stroking the length of hers, sucking, deepening the contact until she moved with him, breathed with him.

He tasted even better than she'd anticipated. Hotter. Sweeter. More intoxicating.

He leaned into her, his chest barely grazing her breasts. But he didn't touch her with his hands, and she didn't touch him. She couldn't. She was paralyzed, lost in a kiss that was more potent than any she'd ever experienced before.

"Hell's bells. I swear I'm stuck smack-dab in the middle of the *Twilight Zone,* 'cause things keep getting stranger by the minute."

Uncle Spur's voice pushed past the loud thud of her heart. She started to pull away, but Austin had heard, as well. He tore his mouth from hers and dragged in a deep breath of air as his gaze swiveled to the old man standing at the corner of the building.

"You've got rotten timing, old man."

"Look at the pot calling the kettle pitch-black. Why, you're the one who keeps running me over with all that rushing here and there, and right when I'm nursing a delicate constitution, and now a sore toe." He limped forward a few steps.

"What happened?"

"This is all your fault. Muffins. I should have known ain't no muffin in the world going to soften up a prickly old pear like Marshalyn."

"She didn't like the muffins?"

"She liked 'em just fine, or so she said, and then I said she could eat to her heart's content and not have to worry about me putting anything funny in them, on account of I can see just fine.''

''You didn't.''

''Didn't what? I just wanted her to know the muffins weren't sabotaged or anything on account of the miserable night that I had. I was sincere.''

''Where is she?''

''Probably down at the corner by now. She was huffing and puffing and walking awful fast when she busted out of the beauty salon after stepping on my toe.''

''Christ, I've got to go after her before she tries to cross the street,'' Austin told Madeline. His gaze collided with hers and he planted another deep, plundering kiss before pulling away. ''We'll finish this later tonight. I'll see you at seven.''

His last words barely registered because the quick assault of his mouth sucked the air from her lungs and scattered all rational thought. She leaned back against the building and tried to catch her breath.

''This is all your fault,'' Spur told her as he limped closer.

''How's that?'' She forced a deep breath and tried to calm her still-pounding heart.

He'd taken the initiative. He'd really and truly *finally* taken the initiative and put the moves on her *first*.

''You made me go in there like some dadburned fool.''

''You were a sweet old man when you went in

there. You didn't turn into a dadburned fool until you opened your mouth.''

"You don't have to look so happy about it.''

"I'm not. It's terrible. Tragic. A waste of good muffins.''

Her happiness came from an entirely different source. She'd done it. She'd pushed Austin to the limit with her newly formulated, hundred-dollar-a-tube, surefire formula guaranteed to drive the nearest man to his breaking point.

Her smile faded.

While she'd anticipated just such a reaction—she'd been counting on it—the reality of it was far less gratifying than the concept.

Because she realized his sudden offensive had nothing to do with her charm or her sex appeal or *her*.

It was simply the lotion.

"I don't think I feel so good,'' Spur grumbled.

"You and me both.''

"WE'VE GOT A HIT,'' Madeline told Duane later that afternoon as she stood in her kitchen, the phone to her ear. "I tried the prototype today and it worked.''

"How many times?''

"Once.''

"Only one test subject? How can you be so sure of the lotion's effectiveness? It could be a fluke. An accident. An—''

"My test subject kissed me. A stubborn, indifferent, determined subject who's obviously completely unattracted to me. Until today.''

"Bull's-eye," Duane said, followed by a low whistle. "And you're convinced it was the lotion?"

Her mind flashed back to the previous night and the determination in his eyes.

He'd been so intent on resisting her.

But today…with the final formula, he'd suddenly made the move first.

It *had* to be the lotion.

"I'm dead certain. I'm sending you what I mixed up this morning and you can distribute it to the trial-and-error team. I'm also e-mailing the formulas for the five various flavors. Hand them over to the rest of the team and let's get some solid data together for next week's presentation."

"I'll get on it first thing Monday morning." The sound of a cork popping echoed over the phone line. "Tonight, it's time to celebrate."

"You're not near a live burner, are you? Alcohol is flammable and—"

"I'm at least three feet away."

"Duane."

"Two and a half at the very least. Look, you need to chill out and relax. Enjoy. We did it! You're going all the way to head of research and development and I'll be right beside you. Your trusted sidekick. The Silver to your Lone Ranger. The Robin to your Batman." A crinkling sounded in the background, followed by a few quick crunches, "The Cheetah to your Tarzan—"

"Are you eating, too?"

"Who?" A gulp punctuated the question. "Of course not."

"Put up the peanuts."

"Peanuts don't go with champagne. They're corn chips."

"I'm not hearing this."

"You know, instead of angsting over my diet, you should go out and find your own bottle of champagne, your own corn chips and a really hot man and do a little celebrating of your own."

*If only.*

But the last thing she felt like doing was celebrating. Besides the only *really* hot man within a five-mile radius wasn't really hot. Not for her, that is. He just thought he was, courtesy of her new product, which she'd dubbed *The Sex Solution.*

She barely ignored the urge to toss the remaining lotion into a nearby trashcan. Instead she squirted a little into her hands and closed her eyes. The lotion tingled, warming as she rubbed it into her skin, the scent filling her nostrils, and a gasp escaped her lips...

Ugh. She opened her eyes to the empty kitchen. Life truly did suck. She'd come so far since leaving Cadillac in the first place, yet here she was back home again, alone on a Friday night with nothing but a refrigerator to satisfy her cravings.

An *empty* refrigerator, except for the various ingredients for her lotion. She stared at a dish of pumpkin-flavored gel and thought of Uncle Spur. Nah. She wasn't that desperate. Yet.

Fifteen minutes later, she pulled a batch of instant

biscuits out of the oven, grabbed a bottle of honey and headed for the sofa. It wasn't an Oreo, but beggars couldn't be choosers and the Piggly Wiggly closed its doors at six o'clock.

Her gaze shifted to the clock that read a half hour until seven. *We'll finish this later tonight. I'll see you at seven.* A thrill of anticipation rippled through her and she had the sudden urge to rush upstairs and wiggle into her man-killer dress.

"You're hopeless," she told herself. "He's not coming."

Once out of range of Madeline and her lotion, his senses had undoubtedly calmed. He'd probably spent the afternoon wondering what had come over him and vowing never, ever to let it happen again.

She grabbed the bottle of honey and squirted a dollop of golden liquid on top of one warm biscuit. Austin Jericho was *not* going to come begging for another kiss, or anything more.

Twinkles, on the other hand, was a different story altogether. The dog sat next to her, a hopeful look on his face. She pinched off a piece and tossed it to him. He caught it, swallowing in one gulp before licking his chops. He eased closer, nuzzling her as he whined, but she shook her head.

"Sorry, boy. I need this a lot more than you do." She popped a bite into her mouth, the honey oozing over her fingers. Sliding a fingertip into her mouth, she licked the honey and went for another bite. Twinkles kept whining and she ended up sharing her biscuit with him. He was a pain, but she had a soft spot for him.

She'd tossed him the very last piece and had just gotten up to go and fetch another when she heard the screen door squeak. She waited for Uncle Spur to push the door open, but instead the doorbell sounded. She opened the door to find Austin Jericho standing on her doorstep a full fifteen minutes before seven.

She could tell that he'd just showered. He wore a white T-shirt that outlined his broad chest and clung to his muscular biceps. Faded jeans cupped his crotch and molded to his thighs. His dark hair was damp, curling around his neck. His five-o'clock shadow was gone, his jaw fresh and clean shaven.

While she'd loved the feel of his stubble rasping against her cheek, she found herself suddenly desperate to feel the masculine smoothness rubbing not only her cheek, but lower, down the slope of her neck, the rise of her breasts, her nipples, the tender insides of her thighs…

She drew a deep breath and tried for a calm tone. "You're early."

"Actually—" he stepped forward, backing her into the small hallway before kicking the door shut with the heel of his boot "—I'm running pretty damned late. This has been a long time coming."

His words sent a thrill of anticipation through her before she reminded herself about his sudden change of heart and the reason behind it. "I agree with you, but it's all wrong."

"It feels pretty damned right."

"I know it does, but that's just because you're not thinking clearly right now."

"Thinking is not at the top of my list right now, sugar. It's all about feeling."

She wanted to dispute his words, but when he looked at her with his hungry gaze, it was as if she'd stepped into her wildest fantasy and the only thing she could manage to do was drag some much-needed air into her lungs.

He glanced past her. "Where's Spur?"

She licked her lips and fought for her voice. "Drowning today's sorrow in a double-dipped cone down at the Dairy Freeze."

"And then?"

*He's coming home.* That's all she had to say to kill the excitement in his eyes and shatter the fantasy.

"Then he's going to bingo," she murmured. She'd dreamed of this moment, fantasized about it for so long that she couldn't bring herself to tell him the truth. No man had ever looked at her quite this way, with this intensity, with this blatant need and it made her feel like...a woman. A real, bona fide, not-too-big-in-the-hips woman. Attractive. Sexy. Wanted. "It's triple-play night and he says that he's due for some good luck after today."

"Good." He flipped the dead bolt on the front door and turned on her, backing her up the few steps to the wall.

"What are you doing?" she asked when he reached for the hem of her T-shirt.

"Undressing you."

"But—wait," she said as he pulled the material up a few dangerous inches, his fingertips brushing her bare skin. Reality zapped her and she realized that this was far from any fantasy and as much as she wanted him, she wanted him to want her. *Her.* "There's something I have to tell you first."

He pulled the shirt up over her head and tossed it to the hardwood floor. His fingers went to the clasp of her bra and her breasts spilled free.

"About this afternoon—"

"You have the most incredible nipples I've ever seen."

"It really wasn't—I do?" She stared up into his dark, heated eyes and saw the admiration. The appreciation. The want.

And suddenly the only thing Madeline Hale could think of was how it would feel to have Austin's mouth on her, regardless of the reason why.

# *12*

---

"I WANTED TO TOUCH THEM so bad last night, and I wanted to taste them. I really wanted to taste them."

Before she could drag in a breath, he dipped his head and drew one sensitive peak into his mouth.

He sucked her so hard and so thoroughly and it was all she could do to keep from sagging against him. Wetness flooded the sensitive flesh between her legs and drenched her panties. He drew on her harder, his jaw creating a powerful tugging that she felt clear to her womb. An echoing throb started in her belly, more intense with every rasp of his tongue, every nibble of his teeth, every pull of his sinful lips.

Heat flowered through her, pulsing along her nerve endings, heating her body until she felt as if she would explode.

He didn't touch her with his hands, just his mouth working at her until she moaned long and low and deep in her throat. Her nipple was red and swollen and throbbing when he finally released her to lick a path to the other breast. The tip of his tongue rasped her ultrasensitive flesh, sending goose bumps up and down her arms and making the hair on the back of her neck stand on end.

"Please," she murmured, and he gladly obliged, seizing the other nipple and delivering the same delicious torture. Pull and nibble and pull and nibble and...

Ahh...

She grew wetter and hotter, her body throbbing with each movement of his mouth as he worked her, pushing her closer to the edge, to a mind-blowing orgasm.

*And at nothing more than having her nipple suckled.*

It didn't make any sense, yet at the same time, it made perfect sense because this wasn't just any man. This was *the* man.

The thought sent a burst of panic through her and she opened her mouth to protest. But then his mouth was on hers, swallowing her words, his hot fingers rolling and plucking her damp nipple, and all thought flew south to the wet heat saturating her panties and the steady, frenzied throbbing between her legs.

He pulled her flush against him, his hands trailing down her bare back, stirring every nerve ending along the way. Fingers played at her waistband before slipping lower, his palms cupping her buttocks through the material. He urged her up on her tiptoes until her pelvis cradled the massive erection straining beneath his zipper.

The feel of him sent a burst of longing through her and suddenly she couldn't get close enough. She grasped his shoulders, clutching at his T-shirt as she wrapped one leg around his thigh to fit more snugly against him. She couldn't get enough of him as she kissed him with all of the passion that had built over the past sleepless nights.

Her tongue danced with his and she sucked, drawing him deeper, wanting more yet not getting enough.

When he tore his lips from hers, a whimper slipped past her swollen lips.

"Don't stop," she gasped. "Please, I don't know what I'll do if you stop." She was pathetic, she knew. Begging a man when she should have been telling him the truth.

Then again, she *was* telling him the God's honest— she needed him more than she needed her next breath.

"I'm not going to stop." His fingers went to the snap on her shorts. The waistband eased and her zipper hissed, and the denim sagged on her hips. Large, eager hands pushed the material down, his fingers snagging the straps of her panties and urging them down, as well. Until she was completely naked. "In fact," he went on, "if I don't get inside of you right now, I'm going to burst."

Satisfaction rushed through her and she smiled.

He caught the expression with his mouth, urging her lips apart in another deep, mind-blowing kiss as he lifted her. He wrapped her legs around his waist, his denim-covered erection flush against the sensitive folds between her legs.

The sudden contact drew a gasp from her lips. She grasped his shoulders and shimmied against him. The friction of the rough material against her clitoris worked her into a frenzy, until she couldn't take any more. She threw her head back as a deep, pleasure-filled moan vibrated up her throat. Delicious tremors racked her body.

"Christ, you're beautiful."

She heard his deep, raw voice through the thunder of her own heart and his words sent a rush of joy through her. She didn't stop to analyze why. Instead, she concentrated on the sincerity in his voice and let it feed the satisfaction gripping her body.

So lost in the throes of her orgasm, she didn't even notice that he'd carried her up the stairs and into her bedroom until she felt the soft mattress at her back.

She glanced up in time to see him peel off his shirt and unfasten his jeans. He shoved the denim and his white briefs down in one smooth motion, his erection springing forward, huge and greedy. A white drop of pearly liquid beaded on the tip and she couldn't help herself, she reached out and touched the moisture, bringing it to her lips to taste the salty sweetness the way she'd tasted it four nights ago.

He groaned at the sight of her before leaning over to reach into his pocket. He pulled out a condom and smoothed it over his throbbing length in one deft motion, and then he was leaning over her, pushing her into the mattress as he urged her legs apart and settled himself between her trembling thighs.

He kissed her then, licking her lips and sucking at her tongue, as if he couldn't get enough of her mouth flavored with his essence.

Her insides were still quivering when he drove into her, burying himself to the hilt with one powerful thrust. She was tight, grasping the full length of him with enough force to make him groan. He lay still for a moment.

"You feel even better than I remember. So tight and wet."

"You feel better, too. Bigger. Hot. Hard." She couldn't believe she'd said the words, but she couldn't help herself. With his voice so deep and stirring in her ears, she found herself eager to give him the same pleasure that he gave her when he said such things.

*Pleasure.* That's what she felt, from her toes clear to the very end of each and every hair on her head. The sensation swamped her, making her feel hot and needy and alive. She closed her eyes, determined to savor every moment. The weight of his body between her legs, the tickle of his hair against her most sensitive spot, the weight of his testicles resting between her thighs.

"Look at me, Maddie." His deep, raw voice drew her eyes open and she stared up.

Hunger blazed hot and intense in his gaze, but there was something else, as well. A possessive light that sent a tremor of warmth through her, as if she were the only woman he'd ever been with. The only woman he'd ever wanted to be with. The first and the last…

"It's Madeline," she murmured in a rush of panic. "Not Maddie. Madeline."

He didn't reply, he simply smiled and started to withdraw. The movement was slow and tantalizing, and her thoughts faded in a wave of pleasure. He stopped just shy of completely pulling out, the head of his penis still nestled just inside.

He pulsed with the force of his desire and she felt him thick at her opening. Before she could draw her next breath, he thrust deep again, sending a burst of heat through her and making her own body throb in response.

He pumped faster with each thrust, driving her toward another orgasm while he worked toward his own. She clutched at him, raking her nails down the length of his back, grasping his buttocks, pulling him deeper as she lifted her pelvis to meet each of his movements. She couldn't feel him deep enough or hard enough or fast enough...

Yet her climax built, lifting her up and jerking her down like a wild roller-coaster ride. Up and down, higher and higher, faster and faster until she finally reached the last peak and raced over the edge, her heart pounding, her blood rushing, her body singing with exhilaration.

She cried out and felt him stiffen. She opened her eyes just in time to see him poised above her. His entire body tensed as he threw his head back, his teeth clenched. Every muscle in his body tightened and bulged as he followed her over that last and final peak.

He rolled onto his back, pulling her on top of him without breaking their contact. His heart pounded against her own and his breaths came sharp and ragged.

Maddie rested her cheek in the curve of his neck and fought for a calming breath. She needed to gather her wits, to think.

Impossible with him so close.

She could only feel. The tickle of his hair against her chafed nipples, the hot slickness of his thigh on the inside of her own, the length of his penis nestled in her slick folds. He was still semihard, the large, smooth head twitching and pulsing against her most sensitive spots with each of his deep, shuddering breaths.

Gathering her courage, she climbed from atop him. He caught her wrist with one large hand, his fingers burning into her as she tried to scramble from the bed.

"Where are you going?"

"I—I need a drink of water."

He stared at her for a long moment, his dark eyes piercing her, looking straight through her and seeing everything she fought so hard to hide. She didn't think he would let her go, but then he released her and she scrambled from the bed.

A few minutes later, she reached the dark safety of the kitchen. She paused, her palms flat against the cool tile as she drew in some much-needed air.

The reality of what had just happened hit her and filled her with a mixture of emotions. Everything from elation to dread. While she'd dreamed of this, she hadn't dreamed of *this*. The pounding of her heart, the buzzing of her nerves, the rush of adrenaline. She felt too alive, more so than when he'd touched her that first night, or the next. Tonight had been different. More intense. Powerful.

Thanks to *The Sex Solution*.

"That went way too fast," he said from behind her.

"I know what you mean."

"We should have slowed down a little."

"My thoughts exactly."

"We skipped too much. I was just so turned-on that I couldn't help myself."

"It was the lotion—" she began, but he cut her off with a press of his fingertips to her lips.

"But that won't happen again because I'll hold on next time. I promise."

"I put the final ingredients together and perfected the product. That's why you were so turned-on tonight. It wasn't really me—next time?"

"*This* time." He lifted her onto the table and reached for the bottle of honey that she'd left out.

She was about to repeat what she'd just said when she felt the cold thickness of the honey trickle down the slope of her breast. She half turned to see his hand poised over her shoulder, the bottle of honey in his hands as he squeezed.

She closed her eyes, savoring the erotic feel of the syrupy liquid sliding, tantalizing her bare skin. Her teeth sank into her bottom lip and her nipples sprang hard and greedy to life. Not fifteen minutes ago, they'd been going after it and here she was up for more action.

And so was he. She could feel his erection pressing into her buttocks. He wanted her again, as much as she wanted him. Maybe more.

Guilt rushed through her. Then again, she'd told him the truth. It wasn't really her fault if he'd decided not to listen. She'd tried.

She would try again, but not right now. She couldn't

find her voice, particularly when his arms came around her to catch a drop of honey and smooth it over her nipple.

Later. Tomorrow. Monday at the latest.

But she *would* bring up the subject again and make sure that he understood. He would call it quits then, she had no doubt, but until then...

She intended to enjoy every sweet, stirring moment of their time together.

MADELINE KNEW Austin was an incredible lover, but over the next week, he went above and beyond anything she'd ever imagined. It wasn't just the way he touched her—his hands so strong and sure and stirring—but the way he made her feel when he touched her.

Feminine. Sexy. Beautiful. *Special.*

Not that she had any delusions about the last one. Austin had always been popular with the ladies for a reason, and now she knew why firsthand.

She leaned up on her elbow and watched him as he moved about the darkened bedroom. His bedroom. A beige-and-navy-blue plaid comforter covered the king-size bed. The walls were paneled a dark, rich oak. A hand-carved dresser sat against the far wall, a matching nightstand just to her right. It looked like him. Simple. Masculine. Powerful.

And it smelled like him.

She drew in a deep breath and let the scent of warm, aroused male fill her nostrils.

For privacy's sake, he'd brought her here after the

honey episode in Cheryl Louise's kitchen. She'd barely recovered from another monumental orgasm when Uncle Spur had knocked on the door. Rather than sneak out the back door like a teenager caught after curfew, Austin had slipped his T-shirt over her head, picked her up and carried her out to his truck, much to Uncle Spur's surprise.

She'd been embarrassed, but the feeling had quickly passed when Austin had driven out of the driveway and pulled her up next to him. With only the T-shirt covering her bare body, she'd felt self-conscious, embarrassed and aroused, all at the same time.

That's what he did to her. Truthfully, he did stir all of the old feelings she'd felt as a naive seventeen-year-old, but there was more. Because she wasn't seventeen. She was a grown woman and she responded like one.

They'd spent all the spare time they could together over the past seven days, in between Austin tending to his cattle and Maddie tending to the dogs and plants. She'd never felt more like a woman in her whole life.

"You're awake." His deep voice drew her from her thoughts and she smiled as he sank down onto the edge of the bed to pull on his boots.

"It's early."

"Early to bed, early to rise."

"We didn't go to bed early. We never got out of bed."

He grinned and leaned over to plant a long, lingering kiss on her already passion-swollen lips. He leaned back and stood up to fasten the button on his jeans. "I won't be able to make it back to the house for lunch. I've got two hundred head being delivered today. I'll be lucky to make it back in time for dinner."

"We'll just have to make up for lunchtime tonight then."

He pulled a T-shirt from the drawer. "Speaking of which, I'll pick you up at seven."

"I can meet you back here. You'll be tired, so you shouldn't have to drive."

"You're on the way, sugar."

"On the way where?"

"The VFW Hall. Tonight's Miss Marshalyn's going-away party."

The enormity of what he was saying sent a burst of joy through her.

Joy?

She forced the silly, naive emotion aside and shook her head. "I've got a lot of packing to do. I can't make it."

He eyed her. "Let me get this straight. You can make time to have sex with me, but you can't find time to go to a party with me."

Not just any party. *The* party because she was *the* woman. His serious-relationship prospect.

"That's exactly what I'm saying." She threw her legs over the side of the bed and reached for her clothes.

"I'm missing something here."

"If I go to the party, then everyone will think there's something going on between us."

He caught her arm and forced her around to face him. "There *is* something going on between us."

"Great sex."

"That and something more."

"There is no more. I'm not your type."

"You're exactly my type."

"Once, a long time ago, but not now. You've sworn off women like me, remember? You said so yourself. You want a good girl, and I no longer qualify."

"You're not a bad girl." At her pointed look, he added, "You have your moments, darlin', I won't deny that. But who you are—" he tapped her chest just above the steady thud of her heart "—in here, is as far from a bad girl as a woman can get. You're not just out for a good time. It's not in your nature. Women like you want more from a man."

"Women like me? For your information, I don't want more from any man. What we have is just fine by me."

"So you're saying you're only attracted to me on a physical level? There's nothing more? No feelings involved? I still remember all that white-knight stuff you wrote in that letter you were too embarrassed to admit to."

"I grew up. I changed."

"You made muffins."

"Uncle Spur was desperate. But I hated every minute of it." Of course, seeing the look of pure ecstasy on Uncle Spur's face when he'd bitten into one had been worth the hour spent slaving away in the hot kitchen. *Almost,* she reminded herself. But then she'd had to clean up.

"You still blush when I touch you."

"I have overactive skin pigmentation. It's a medical condition."

"You still tremble, for Chrissake."

She shrugged. "I have low blood pressure. I tremble all the time." She gave a loud *burrr.* "In fact, I'm cold right now."

"You're scared."

"I am not scared."

"You're scared that if you go to the party with me tonight, you'll find out that you're a lot more like the girl you used to be than you want to admit. That you actually like it here. That you haven't outgrown this place, despite your big-city ties. That you still fit."

"I do not fit."

"You fit, all right. You haven't changed, not one bit."

"I have, too."

"Have not. You're still afraid to show your feelings. Afraid for people to see inside you. You haven't changed. You're still running from your feelings now, just like you were back then."

"I don't know what you're talking about."

"You're running from your feelings for Sharon the way you ran from your feelings for me. You won't talk about her or look at pictures or even think about her because you're afraid it will hurt. Just like you wouldn't own up to that love letter. You were afraid to get hurt."

"You're wrong."

"And you're afraid, all right. You're afraid that you might fall for me all over again if you give yourself a chance."

"And you're afraid not to fall for me."

"How's that?"

"While I've changed—and I *have* changed—I'll admit that a lot of people in this town don't think so. In fact, most of the people in this town still think I'm little Maddie, Miss Marshalyn included."

"What are you trying to say?"

"That you want to keep your promise, and in order to do that, you have to show up with a serious prospect tonight. While I'm far from the right person for the job, as far as this town goes, I'm just what the doctor ordered. I'm your ticket to success," she said, now fully dressed.

"Is that what you really think? That I would use you to get Miss Marshalyn's land because people still perceive you as the same nice, wholesome small-town girl who left here twelve years ago?" He sounded so hurt that her chest tightened.

"I think that we have great sex and you're using that as a basis for a real relationship because you need one to keep from losing the closest thing to a real home that you've ever had."

"You're full of shit."

"I don't blame you," she went on. "People get married for a lot less these days. In fact, most would be completely happy to find a great sex match. But the physical connection is as much a false perception as I am. It's the lotion stirring your senses, making you so hot and turned-on that you can't see straight."

"You're wrong."

She shook her head, grabbed her purse and walked away before she did something really stupid, like throw herself into his arms and kiss him until the hurt faded from his expression.

That would imply that Madeline Hale cared about more than sex with Austin Jericho. That she actually cared about him. That she truly had fallen for him all over again, and fallen hard.

But she wouldn't.

Not ever again.

# 13

MADELINE WAS NOT RUNNING from anything.

She was running *to* something, she told herself later that day as she packed up the last of her work paraphernalia and headed upstairs to pack her personal belongings.

She had a blossoming career and a great big fat promotion waiting for her back in Houston, along with her condo and her furniture and the life she'd built for herself.

Running, of all the crazy, ridiculous things...

The thought faded into a familiar wave of panic as she started to pass Sharon's room. She quickened her steps and fixed her gaze straight ahead, and that's when reality hit her.

*Running.*

She came to a dead stop and simply stood there for a long moment, her heart pounding, panic so real and palpable that she could taste it in her mouth.

*Afraid.*

As she stood there staring at the closed door, she realized that Austin was right. She was running from the past, avoiding any and all mention of Sharon, terrified of any reminders of her dear, sweet friend because they also brought back the pain she'd felt.

Pain she'd left behind twelve years ago as she'd rolled out of town in her little Pinto.

But it was still there. Still stalking her. She felt it every time she thought of home. Every time she saw a flower-print dress or drank an ice-cream soda or watched a rerun of *Laverne and Shirley*. It had followed her to Dallas, and it had followed her back here.

But it wasn't merely dogging her. It lived and breathed inside of her.

The fear controlled her.

"No," she murmured, reaching for the doorknob before she lost her nerve.

Her heart stalled as the door creaked open. She flipped on the light switch and forced herself inside.

The walls were still painted the same shade of lipstick-pink that had always been Sharon's favorite. A Van Halen poster graced one wall, next to Madonna in her early days. In the midst of the pop icons stood a very young looking George Strait playing his guitar.

The furniture was white, the bed sporting a matching lipstick-pink canopy. A makeup vanity sat just to the right, covered with various tubes and bottles just the way it had been so long ago.

Maddie had been inside here so many times with Sharon, sprawled across the bed on a rainy Saturday afternoon, or sitting Indian-style in the middle of the furry pink rug with her homework in her lap.

This room was familiar, not frightening. That's what Madeline told herself as she walked its perimeter. She touched Sharon's things, from stuffed animals to science trophies to a pair of daisy-print flip-flops that still sat in the far corner of the room, and she let the memories come.

They played through her mind and made her smile until she reached Sharon's nightstand and she saw a silver-framed picture.

A graduation picture taken the day of the accident.

They'd been on their way back from the photographer's in Sharon's new graduation present. Sarah was supposed to be with them, but she'd gotten grounded for missing her curfew the night before and so it had just been Sharon and Madeline. Madeline had begged to drive. She'd never been behind the wheel of an automatic. Just her old, clunky standard Pinto and she'd been in awe of the brand-new car.

Sharon had agreed and they'd climbed over each other to switch seats. They'd gone riding then and Madeline had fallen even more in love with the car. They'd burned a tank of gas by the time the sun had set and they'd finally started home.

She closed her eyes and remembered the cool wind rushing at her face as she'd pressed the gas and headed down the back road toward town. She'd been going too fast, but it had been so easy. The car rode so smoothly she hadn't even realized the speed until it had been too late.

The deer had appeared right in the middle of the road and she'd swerved to avoid hitting the animal. She'd hit the shoulder and a great big pothole instead. The car had skidded toward the ditch and she'd yanked on the steering wheel. The car kept skidding before rolling onto its side with a bone-jarring force that had made her teeth ache.

But that's all she'd felt. Just the pain of being tossed around and ramming to a halt. No permanent injuries, but when she'd looked over at her friend…

Maddie's eyes popped open, trading the memory in favor of the picture that sat on the nightstand. Guilt rushed through her, making her heart pound and her chest tighten, but she didn't run away.

Not this time.

She forced her hand out and picked up the picture. Settling on the edge of the bed, she stared into her friend's face. But she didn't see the smiling girl in the blue cap and gown, she saw the blood and the pain and the desperate blue eyes of the girl trapped in the passenger's seat. The dashboard had caved in, crushing Sharon's legs and pinning her in place.

Thanks to the steering wheel, Maddie had been unharmed. She'd stumbled from the car and flagged down the first car that came down the road, and then she'd climbed back into the car to wait for help with Sharon. She'd talked and told her friend to hold on, but it hadn't been enough. Sharon had died before the ambulance had rolled up. And Maddie had lived.

But while she'd lived, she hadn't lived up to the promise she'd made to Sharon as she'd sat crushed in the car. *No regrets.* Because Maddie still nursed the biggest regret of all.

"It should have been me," she whispered.

But it hadn't been. As much as she'd hated that fact,

she'd been thankful, too. She'd been young and terrified of death.

Survival had come at its own cost, however. She'd felt not only the loss of her closest and dearest friend, but guilt, as well.

And so she'd run away, racing out of town under the pretense of following her dreams. She'd been determined to leave behind the scared girl who'd sat in the demolished car and tried to comfort Sharon during those last few moments.

But that girl hadn't stayed behind in Cadillac. She'd followed, burying herself deep inside the confident woman who'd gone out to seek her fortune, hiding along with the nearly overwhelming guilt and grief and fear.

No more.

Maddie clutched the picture to her chest, closed her eyes and let the image of that night come to her. For the first time since she'd held the dying girl in her arms, she cried.

And with each tear that rolled down her cheeks, the pain in her chest started to ease.

"I LIKE HER." Miss Marshalyn's voice drew Austin around to see the woman who'd come up beside him. She was staring across the dance floor at the petite redhead who was serving punch.

Debbie the kindergarten teacher.

He'd finally narrowed down his handful of choices and picked the first one on the list—the only respectable woman Austin Jericho had had more than two dates with in the past few years.

Three, to be exact, including this one.

The other two had come before Maddie Hale had walked back into his life.

"I really like her."

"I don't." He turned toward the older woman who'd been like a mother to him for most of his hell-raising life. She'd never passed judgment, never condemned him. She'd merely stated her opinion and given him a choice. A chance.

Tonight was another chance, but one he couldn't take.

"I mean, I do like her. She's nice. Sweet. She loves kids. She'll make someone a great wife. But not me." He shook his head. "I just brought her tonight because I knew you would like her."

"So you're saying that you broke your promise."

"I'm saying that I want your land, but I won't take it by being dishonest. To you or myself. And that's what I would be if I let you think there could possibly be a future between me and Debbie. She's not my type."

He'd accused Maddie of running from the past, but he was just as guilty. He was running from his own past, from the old Austin Jericho who'd had nothing to call his own. No home.

He *was* afraid of losing Miss Marshalyn's land, but at the same time, he was more afraid of losing Maddie Hale. The thought of her rolling out of town still believing that he wasn't genuinely attracted to her made him feel sick inside.

"Maybe Houston will show up and make you proud."

"You make me proud, Austin Jericho. You always have. You can have the land. I didn't mean to force you into something you didn't want to do. I just think you need to find the right woman and settle down."

"Sometimes it's not that simple. Sometimes the right woman is also a damned stubborn one."

"Amen to that." Spur's voice sounded behind them and they both turned to see the old man, hat in one hand and a bouquet of wildflowers in the other.

Miss Marshalyn frowned. "Are you calling me stubborn, Spur Tucker?"

"I sure as hell am, and I'm also calling you the right woman. My woman." He shrugged. "I know I don't always say the right things. Hell, I don't know what's right or wrong half the time. But I can promise I'll always speak the truth and honesty's got to count for something. The fact that I like you more than my horse, Miss Daisy, has to count for something, too. Otherwise I give up on this courting business 'cause it ain't worth a hog's ass—"

"I like you, too."

"—and I might as well stick to my solitude—you what?"

"I like you, too." She smiled and took the flowers. "Most of the time, that is, but nobody's perfect."

"Damn straight. You're about as blind as an old bat."

"I really don't like you right now."

"A situation easily fixed," Austin reminded her. "The doc wants to do surgery."

"I don't like surgery or hospitals or any of the like."

"I had a hernia surgery last year. It was a piece of cake," Spur told them. "Except for the food. If I hadn't been a sick man, I would have been ailin' something fierce after eating that slop. And then there was the pain. It hurt something fierce."

"I really, *really* don't like you right now."

"It'll pass." He grinned. "Come on, darlin'. Let's go get some refreshments and talk about your surgery. Why, I bet we could pack you a few lunches and beg the doc for an extra few painkillers and you'd be sittin' pretty."

"I'm not packing anything or begging for painkillers because I'm not having the surgery."

"Of course you ain't." He took her arm. "But if you don't, you're liable to trip walking down the aisle when we finally tie the knot—"

"*If* we tie the knot," she cut in.

"And how would that look to all those auxiliary biddies who love to gossip," he went on as if she hadn't said a word.

"I can see you two have things to talk about." Austin kissed the old woman on the cheek. "I'll see you later."

"Where are you going?"

"I've got something I need to do."

It wasn't just a night of truth for Austin. Maddie

had a few of her own to face before she moved out of town and out of his life.

Starting right now.

"IT'S THE LAST SUPPER, girl." Madeline fed Twinkles the biscuit she'd stuffed into her pocket and scratched the dog behind the ears. The animal whimpered. "Not *the* last supper. Our last one together. Are you going to miss me?" Twinkles gave her an affectionate nudge before shoving her nose near Madeline's pocket and sniffing. "I'd like to think it's me, but I know better than that." She stood and tugged at the dog's leash, leading the animal back home after their nightly walk.

She'd stayed out a half hour longer tonight, not half as eager as she usually was for the walk to end. She was going to miss Twinkles.

The animal jerked on the leash and tried to pull Maddie off in a different direction and it was all she could do to hold on and keep the direction for home. Fifteen minutes later when she'd finally reached the dark house, her shoulder screamed from the effort.

After tonight, there would be no racing around after an animal that had more energy than a hyper five-year-old, no endless vacuuming morning and night.

Okay, so maybe she wasn't going to miss Twinkles all that much.

"This way, girl." She tugged her up onto the porch and reached for the doorknob. That's when she noticed the rear bumper of Austin's truck just off to the side of the house, the chrome gleaming in the moonlight.

Her heart skipped its next beat as she reached for the doorknob.

"Austin?" she called as she stepped in. No voice greeted her as she bent down to unclip the leash.

The dog rushed toward the kitchen and her doggie bowl while Madeline turned toward the staircase.

She saw the familiar boots sitting at the bottom of the stairs. A few steps up, she saw a faded pair of denim jeans, the edges frayed and worn. Another couple of steps and a white T-shirt lay in a heap.

A thrill ran through her as she mounted the steps. She paused to pick up the shirt and lift it to her nose. The familiar scent of Austin Jericho filled her nostrils and brought tears to her eyes.

Tears?

She fought back the ridiculous notion. Excitement, yes. Austin was the king when it came to turning her on, but Madeline wasn't about to feel anything more.

She wasn't falling for him again.

The trouble was, she had the sinking feeling that she'd already fallen. And when she saw the nude man standing in the shower, she knew it was true.

As she stood there, just two feet away, staring at his powerful, naked body, she didn't think about how much she wanted to touch or kiss or make love to him. The only thing she could think of was how much she wanted to tell him she was sorry for what she'd said that afternoon, sorry for denying her feelings for so long, sorry for leaving him.

Instead, she murmured, "You really shouldn't be here."

He pushed the curtain back. "You said you could make time for sex. I'm here, so make time."

Challenge gleamed in his eyes and she realized that it went beyond just finding a few hours. He was daring her to live up to her words, to prove that everything she'd said had been true that afternoon.

That their connection didn't go beyond sex.

She reached down and pulled the hem of her shirt up over her head, letting the material fall to the floor beside her. She reached for the clasp on her bra, but he beat her to it, his long, tanned fingers reaching out to flick at the front clasp.

The lace of her bra snagged on one nipple, holding the cup in place. She started to shove it aside, but he stopped her. He fingered her through the lace, touching the ripe tip, coaxing it to an even greater awareness. He hauled her closer and dipped his head. Flicking out his tongue, he licked her as if she were his favorite flavor of ice cream. Over and over. Side to side. Up and down.

Finally he pulled the bra loose and tossed it aside. He stepped out of the shower and dropped to his knees to unfasten her shorts and tug the material down her legs. When she stood before him wearing nothing but her panties, he stopped again and stared at her femininity barely concealed by a skimpy pair of panties. Blond hair curled through the lace and he trailed his fingertip over the gold silk, barely touching her. But the motion was more stirring than if he'd shoved his hands into her panties and parted her wet folds.

He stroked softly until she grasped his damp shoulders to keep her legs from buckling beneath her. He leaned closer, his hot, moist breath fanning her, stirring her, making her lean on him all the more for support. He trailed his tongue over the wet material between her legs, pushing the fabric inside her ever so slightly before tracing the edge where skin met elastic. Before she could catch her next breath, he pulled her panties down and hooked one leg over his broad shoulder.

His tongue rasped her then and heat flooded her body, making her burn so hot she thought she would surely melt.

She didn't.

Instead, she stared down at the dark head at her waist and watched in fascination as he touched his mouth to her most intimate flesh and drew her throbbing clitoris between his lips.

She closed her eyes and held on as he suckled and teased and tongued until she couldn't stand it anymore. A long, throaty moan escaped her as her climax hit her. She threw her head back and braced her arms on his broad shoulders as tremor after tremor racked her sweat-drenched body.

Several long seconds passed before her grip on him eased. He kissed her inner thigh and lifted her leg off his shoulder.

Then he stood and swept her into his arms, lifting her over the edge of the clawfoot tub and stepping into the hot spray of the shower. Putting his back to the onslaught of water, he released her legs, letting her slide down the hard, aroused length of his body until her feet met the hard porcelain.

His gaze met hers and never left as he soaped his hands. Soap-slippery fingers slid over her shoulders, circled her breasts and trailed down her abdomen.

She wouldn't think it possible that she could be aroused again so quickly after such an intense orgasm moments before, but at the first touch of his slick hand between her legs, she felt the familiar ache start all over again.

Her focus dropped to his penis. He was long and thick and powerfully aroused and she wanted to touch him more than she wanted her next breath.

She reached down and clasped the velvet-covered steel. His sharp intake of breath echoed off the tile walls and she moved her hand, running it along his length from root to tip and back down again.

He closed his eyes, clearly relishing the sensation as she stroked him. But then his gaze snagged hers and his hand stilled her movements.

"Not yet." He dropped to his knees again and reached for the soap.

For the next several minutes, as Austin smoothed the lather over her body, she discovered how truly amazing a man's touch could be. Relaxing yet stirring at the same time.

By the time he'd rinsed every sudsy drop from her sensitive skin and toweled her dry, she was *this* close to having another orgasm.

But she wouldn't. Not without him. She reached out and stroked his massive penis. She'd never seen a man so big. It was as if the hot shower had stirred him even more. He pulsed beneath her attention, the length of him trembling when she reached out to run her finger over one bulging vein.

He groaned and swept her up into his arms. Several long, powerful strides later, he eased her down onto the mattress and followed, parting her legs and sinking in with a desperation that sent a surge of feminine power through her.

"It's not the lotion," he murmured. "There isn't a drop of it on you now and I'm so hard I can't see straight."

Before the enormity of his words could hit her, he started to move, thrusting into her over and over in a frenzied rhythm. He was out of control, his movements so intense it was almost painful as he pushed them both toward a raging climax. Almost there. She lifted her pelvis, meeting each of his movements and relishing the rush of sensation it stirred.

He came first, his raw, throaty moan filling her ears and pulling her along with him. She quickly followed with a loud scream, her already ravaged senses exploding in a blinding orgasm that left her spent and listless for the next several moments.

It was only when she felt his warm body slide away from her that she managed to lift her head. She looked up to see him poised in the doorway.

"It's you," he murmured, and then he turned and walked away.

The realization of what the shower had meant hit her full force and the air stalled in her lungs. There'd been no lotion stirring his senses, driving him into a lustful frenzy tonight. He'd been hot and hard and desperate, and all because of her.

"Austin, don't—" she scrambled to her feet "—don't go," but her plea came too late.

She reached the bedroom doorway just as she heard the front door slam shut. A few seconds later, his truck fired to life.

He drove away then and Maddie Hale was left with nothing but the truth to keep her company during the long, restless night that followed.

# 14

"WELL, WELL, if it isn't little Maddie Hale."

Maddie smiled at Mayor Ben Skeeter who stood behind the pharmacist's counter at the drugstore wearing a white lab coat and a Houston Astros baseball cap. Like his wife, he wore a campaign button pinned to his lab coat with his picture on it, his with simply *Reelect Mayor Skeeter* printed around the edges.

"What can I do you for today, little lady?" he asked as she walked up to the counter.

"I need the biggest bottle of No-Doz that you've got." She stifled a yawn and pulled her wallet from her purse.

"It looks to me like you need a good night's sleep a heck of a lot more."

"That, too, but it's not a possibility right now. Cheryl Louise just got back from her honeymoon this morning, so I'm headed back to Dallas today and I've got a long drive ahead."

"We'll be sorry to see you go. Camille was so glad to have you back in town. Said seeing you again was like a brush with a major celebrity."

Maddie smiled. "I'm really sorry to hear about her lung cancer. I hope everything goes well."

"We're optimistic because the doctors caught it in time. They say she's got a ninety-five percent chance of a complete recovery once the surgery and chemo treatments are complete. It'll just be a little rough in the meantime."

"Give her my love and tell her I'm thinking about her. Speaking of which, I've got something for her." She fished several sample tubes of *The Sex Solution* from her purse. "Tell her this isn't going out to the public for another six months. She gets first dibs."

"Why, mighty obliged. I know she'll love them. She's got bottles and tubes all over the house at home. A cosmetic junkie, that's what I call her. Oh, I almost forgot." He pulled the cap off his head and slid it across the counter toward her along with a black marker. "I would be really appreciative if you could give me your John Hancock. I'm asking everyone who comes into the store to sign it for her. I thought it might make her feel a little less isolated since she can't come in herself right now. If she sees who comes and goes, she might actually feel like she's here. Besides, she loves the Astros."

Maddie signed the hat and slid it back across the counter.

Her attention was riveted on his shiny bald head before dropping to the election button that bore his image. He sported a full head of salt and pepper hair on the button.

He grinned and rubbed the top of his scalp. "This is for Camille, too. She had her first chemo treatment a few days ago and her hair's already started to fall out. I didn't want her to feel so self-conscious, so I shaved mine off. She laughed so hard when she saw me that I think she actually forgot about her own for a few minutes. She said my head could double for her bowling ball.''

Maddie grinned. "It sounds like you're keeping her spirits up."

"It's the least I can do. For the past forty-eight years that little lady has been busting her tail for me, working twenty-four/seven here at the drugstore while I see to my commitments in town. She's never complained either. She says that's what marriage is all about—teamwork." He plopped the cap back on his head.

"Here you go." Maddie slid a five across the countertop as he bagged up her No-Doz.

"Your money's no good here." He handed her the bag and winked. "You have a safe trip. We'll all miss you."

Not half as much as Maddie was going to miss everyone. She wouldn't have admitted as much two weeks ago, but things had changed since then.

Madeline Hale had finally stopped running from her past and come home. She'd faced her grief and her guilt and her fear, and she'd survived.

Thanks to Austin.

His image appeared in her mind the way he'd been last night, his dark, powerful form standing in the bedroom doorway, his dark eyes glittering in the moonlight.

*"It's you."*

His deep voice echoed through her head and stirred a pang of longing so intense she wanted to cry.

But she'd cried too much already last night. She'd tossed and turned and agonized as she'd faced the fact that he'd spoken the truth.

She believed him, but however much she wanted to stay, she couldn't. Even though she'd fallen helplessly in love with him.

*Because* she'd fallen in love.

She'd tried to convince herself these past years that she'd traded her small-town, boring existence for big-city life complete with parties and concerts and excitement because she actually *liked* all that stuff. No more. She was through pretending to be something she wasn't.

No more running from her past, from the shy, wistful, unsophisticated romantic who'd written sappy love letters and fantasized about happily-ever-afters.

While she'd matured and learned to look at the world from a sophisticated perspective, deep down she was still every bit that young romantic. Sex was fine. Great. But it wasn't enough. She not only wanted the hot nights, she wanted the morning afters. The good times and the not-so-good times. She wanted a man who would tell her how beautiful she was even if she'd lost all her hair. A man who loved her enough to shave *his* hair just so she would feel a little less lonely.

She wanted love. Real, true, till-death-do-us-part, forever and ever *love*.

While she knew Austin had genuine feelings for

her—the physical attraction between them blazed hotter than anything she'd ever felt before—he'd never once mentioned the *L* word.

*Stay.* That's all he'd said. But he hadn't said why. He hadn't given her one good reason, except that they had great chemistry.

While the sexy, confident woman she'd become wanted desperately to stay and see if the chemistry would lead to more, the shy, insecure girl that still lived and breathed inside her wouldn't allow it.

While she'd been fortunate enough to see her fantasy turn into reality for a few hot, steamy nights, deep down she feared that was the most she could ever hope for. She'd learned a long time ago that shy, naive, geeky good girls never ended up with hot, hunky bad boys like Austin Jericho.

Only in her most private fantasies.

She would rather leave now with her memories than stay and see the lust fade.

That would be like watching Austin walk away from her at the football game that time, straight to Big Boobs Barbara. He'd killed her ego that night and Maddie wasn't about to hang around and risk another crushing blow.

Particularly since she had something much more precious than pride at stake this time. She had her heart.

"I'M NOT SELLING you my land."

Austin glanced over his shoulder to see Miss Marshalyn standing behind him. With her conservative yellow pantsuit and her white patent-leather handbag, she looked as if she should be at an afternoon tea rather than smack-dab in the middle of Cherry Blossom Junction on a rocking Friday night.

"I didn't think you would." He took a sip of the beer he'd been nursing for the past few hours since calling it a day at the ranch and heading here rather than his house. A routine he'd started after discovering that Maddie Hale had left town without so much as a goodbye.

Of course, he'd had more than one beer that first night. He'd had more than he could count, but it still hadn't been enough to kill the memory of her in his arms. His bed. His life.

He'd ended up with a vicious hangover the next day, but it hadn't stopped him from coming back that night. He'd stayed within his one-beer limit, however, having already learned the night before that he couldn't drown her memory.

But he could do his damnedest to avoid it, and so he'd kept coming back, trading the quiet solitude of his house for the blaring country music and neon-lit surroundings.

He'd backslid into his earlier days, or so Miss Marshalyn probably thought since he was spending his free time at his old haunt rather than cruising for a potential wife. He didn't blame her. By all appearances, he looked like a man who no longer gave a shit about anyone or anything.

He ran a hand over his face. A week's worth of stubble scraped across his palm. Not that he particularly cared about his appearance, but he hated disappointing her.

Try as he might, he couldn't seem to muster enthusiasm for anything except his work. From sunup to sundown, he busted his ass back at the ranch.

But from sundown to sunup, all he could do was think. Remember.

Christ, he still couldn't believe it. She'd actually *left*.

"I'm not selling it to you," the old woman repeated, pulling him from his thoughts. "I'm giving it to you."

"I don't expect—you're *what?*" He forgot his next sip of beer and swiveled around in time to see her pull a blue-bound contract from her white patent-leather handbag. She plopped it down on the bar next to him.

"It's yours. One hundred acres."

"But I didn't show up at the party with a serious prospect. Hell, I don't even have one. And no prospect means no land."

"My proposition wasn't really about you finding a wife. All I ever wanted for my own peace of mind was to know that you've really grown up. That I don't have to worry and wonder what's going to happen to you. I figured that if you had a nice woman beside you, she could look after you the way I have all these years." She smiled and her eyes brightened with tears. "But you don't need anyone to look after you. You *have* grown up. You proved that to me by being honest. You earned that land. It's yours."

"I don't know what to say." He stared at the deed that now bore his name. *His.* Free and clear.

Surprisingly it didn't bring the rush he'd expected. As he stared down at the one and only thing that had motivated him for the past several years—the hunger to have a real home—he realized that his feelings had changed. Because it wasn't the one and only thing that mattered to him anymore.

Christ, it didn't matter to him half as much as Maddie and the fact that she'd left him.

"I'm curious," Miss Marshalyn went on. "Were you just as honest with Maddie?"

He folded the deed and set it back down on the bar top. "What are you talking about?"

"Did you tell her the truth?"

"She already knew that I needed a serious prospect for your party."

"Not that truth. Did you tell her that you love her?"

"I told her to stay."

"But did you tell her that you *love* her?"

He hadn't. Such a declaration didn't come easy to a man who'd heard those words so sparingly while growing up.

He loved his brothers and they loved him, but none of them sat around saying it to one another. They just knew because they'd weathered the rough times together. They'd made it through a hellish childhood, and they were still here. Still alive. Still supportive of one another.

But the words had never been necessary.

Until now.

"What if she doesn't feel the same way?"

"What if she does? You'll never know if you sit here and keep this bar stool warm. Besides, I'd like to sit down myself and have a farewell drink. Spur and I are leaving first thing in the morning for his ranch and I might not get another chance to say goodbye to my old haunt."

"Your old haunt?"

"I was young once, too, you know, and this place has been around a heck of a long time."

He grinned and turned over his seat.

"By the way, Spur is out in the car waiting. Can you tell him to park and come on in? I'm feeling pretty nostalgic tonight. I think I might like a farewell dance to go with my drink."

Austin kissed her cheek and signaled the bartender to bring her anything she wanted on him. "He better be good to you."

"Oh, he'll be good, all right—otherwise I'll make his life miserable."

"I heard that." Spur's voice sounded behind Austin and he turned to find the old man standing there, his cowboy hat in his hands and car keys in the other.

"Make her happy," he told the older man.

"Don't you worry about that. If there's one thing I've learned about women over the past few weeks, it's this—it's not only what you do, it's what you say."

"Let's hope so," Austin said as he stuffed the deed into his pocket and headed for the door.

Because he wasn't just going to show Maddie how he felt this time, he was going to tell her.

"YOU'RE CRAZY." Duane leaned on the edge of Maddie's desk and folded his arms, a frown on his face. "A genius, but still damned certifiable."

"People change jobs all the time. It doesn't qualify them for the funny farm."

"It does if they've just gotten a nice, big fat promotion, *and* a penthouse office complete with a fully stocked minibar." Duane's stomach grumbled. "Just think, you'll never have to fight with the lunchroom candy machine ever again."

"Has anyone ever told you that you have twisted priorities?"

"My mom, my dad, my sisters, my friends." He nodded. "Pretty much everyone."

Maddie upended a desk drawer into one of the boxes she'd brought in that morning. "I'm leaving, Duane, despite the minibar."

"If it's about the lab…" His gaze shifted to the far corner and the charred remains of what had once been three storage cabinets. Duane had inadvertently set a small fire while munching peanuts and celebrating with champagne much too close to a hot petri dish. "I take full responsibility and I plan on working overtime every night until all the damage is paid for."

"Desiree is so excited about *The Sex Solution* that she couldn't care less about the lab." He breathed a sigh of relief and Maddie eyed him. "But don't get too comfortable. If it happens again, she's liable to snatch away your promotion and send you down to the mailroom for the next six months."

"Trust me. I've learned my lesson."

"Where have I heard that before?" She reached for another cardboard box and upended the second drawer.

"You know," he told her, "marketing is more jazzed about this product than anything V.A.M.P.'s ever done. They say it's not only a great cosmetic, but it has medicinal qualities. They plan on promoting it as a nonpharmaceutical alternative to aiding a low libido."

"They can do whatever they want. It's theirs now."

"Please don't go," Duane finally said after watching her empty drawer number three. "I like working with you. You nag more than my mom, but I need that to keep me in line." It was the most sensible argument he'd made all day since she'd announced her intentions to leave.

"I'm sure whoever Desiree finds to replace me will nag you accordingly, and if they don't, just have them give me a call and I'll set them straight."

"Where are you going?"

"Home right now." She finished with the last of the boxes, handed Duane a few while she took some and started for the hallway.

"You know what I mean."

"When I figure it out, I'll let you know." She hugged him, climbed into her car and drove out of the parking garage onto a busy thoroughfare.

The traffic was horrible as usual and she found herself starting and stopping and thinking about Duane's question.

She knew where she *wanted* to go. Where she belonged. But that wasn't a possibility with Austin Jericho only a few miles away. It had been hard enough to leave in the first place. A decision she'd thought and rethought over the past week since returning to Dallas.

*Take a chance.*

That's what her heart kept telling her, but her common sense knew better. She'd done the right thing, even if it didn't feel so right.

It took her forty-five minutes to make the ten-mile drive to her apartment near the Galleria. After pulling into her parking space, she killed the engine, climbed from behind the wheel and headed for the elevators. She had plenty of time to haul her boxes out of the car tomorrow while she debated what to do next.

After the day she'd had, the only thing on her mind was the extralarge bag of Oreos she'd left sitting on her kitchen counter that morning. A little soothing chocolate and maybe she could actually think.

Of course, she'd scarfed for the past three days and still hadn't been able to come up with the next step for her life. The Oreos didn't seem to be working.

But Maddie had few options right now and so she intended to give them another try.

The moment she opened her front door, she tossed her purse and keys onto a nearby table and headed for the kitchen. She'd just popped a cookie into her mouth when she heard the steady stream of the shower coming from the bathroom down the hall.

Fear rushed through her until she noticed the worn straw Resistol sitting on her kitchen table.

It couldn't be.

That's what she told herself, but as she walked toward the bathroom, her denial turned to heart-pounding excitement. She passed the familiar brown boots, a faded pair of jeans, a black T-shirt imprinted with the slogan Cowboy Up.

Clouds of steam billowed from the open bathroom doorway, nearly obliterating the pair of white cotton briefs resting in the threshold.

She knew it was him even before she stepped into the misty bathroom and saw the naked man standing in her shower.

She blinked once, twice. But he didn't disappear. He was still there on the other side of the glass shower door. Still naked. Still *Austin*.

He rubbed a bar of soap between his hands before running the lather over his chest, his six-pack abs and down over the sprinkle of hair that led to his crotch.

She was riveted by the sight of him for a long, breathless moment before her gaze snapped back up to find him staring straight at her. Desire burned bright, but there was something else, as well.

*It couldn't be.*

Denial raged through her, along with a burst of hope that maybe, just maybe, he felt the same way that she did.

There was only one way to find out.

She slid the glass door to the side. Steam rushed out at her.

"I—" She licked her lips. "How did you get in here?"

"I picked up a few tricks in my bad-boy days."

"What are you doing here?"

A twinkling blue gaze caught and held hers. "Taking a shower."

"I see that. I mean, why?"

"I needed a shower after the drive I just had. Christ, do you know it took me two hours just to get from one end of this town to the next?"

"The traffic's pretty bad."

"It's terrible. It's good that I'm a patient man."

"You? Patient?"

"I must be. I've been waiting on you for over twelve years."

"What's that supposed to mean?"

"It means that I was wrong the other day. I shouldn't have pulled you into the shower without saying a few things first."

"Such as?"

"You turn me on, but you do more than that. You make me happy, Maddie. You make me smile. You make me laugh. You make me better." At her puzzled look, he added, "You were right. I was scared of losing Miss Marshalyn's land. I even went as far as to take Debbie the kindergarten teacher to the party." He shook his head. "But I couldn't go through with it. I couldn't let Miss Marshalyn think there was even a chance of me having a relationship with Debbie. I told her the truth.''

"You gave up the land.'' The realization of what he'd done sent a burst of joy through her.

"You're the only one I want to have a future with,'' he went on. "I love you, Maddie. That's why I'm here. Why I'm staying here.''

"What about your ranch? Your home?''

He shrugged. "Home is where the heart is, sugar, and my heart's here with you. If you want it.''

No sooner were the words out of his mouth than she shrugged out of her jacket, pulled her silk shell over her head and peeled of her skirt. A few seconds later, she threw herself into his arms, kissing him hungrily, drinking in the taste and the scent and the feel of Austin Jericho.

"I really missed you.''

He smiled against her mouth. "Does that mean that you want it? My heart, that is.''

"Yes,'' she breathed in between kisses. "I want it more than you can imagine, but not like this.'' She shook her head and pulled away. "You can't stay here.''

He frowned. "What's that supposed to mean?''

"*We* can't stay here.'' She smiled. "I quit my job today. I love making things, but doing it here in Dallas—'' she shook her head "—this wasn't my dream. Sharon was the one who wanted out of Cadillac. When she passed away, I needed to escape so bad and my guilt was so great that I convinced myself that her dreams were my own. They weren't. I don't belong here. I don't want to belong here."

"Are you saying what I think you're saying?"

She nodded. "I want to bake muffins in my dad's shop. Not that I won't continue with product development for V.A.M.P. I really like perfecting all of those seductive products, especially with such a good test subject." She cupped his face. "I want to do contract work for V.A.M.P. on the side and reopen Sweet & Simple."

"That's what you really want?"

"Actually, you're what I *really* want. Now and forever. And I want to go home. To *our* home." And then she did the one thing she'd wanted to do for the past twelve years—since she'd written that silly note—but never had the courage to.

She stared into his eyes and told him the truth. "I love you, Austin Jericho. I always have and I always will." And then she reached out to show him just how much.

\* \* \* \* \*

*Wait! It's not over yet!*
*Don't miss the fireworks next*
*month when brother Houston*
*finally meets his match in*
*Blaze 131, THE FANTASY FACTOR.*

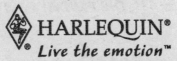

**HARLEQUIN® *Blaze*™**

In April, bestselling author

# Tori Carrington

introduces a provocative miniseries
that gives new meaning to the word *scandal!*

# *Sleeping with Secrets*

Don't miss
**FORBIDDEN** April 2004
**INDECENT** June 2004
**WICKED** August 2004

## *Sleeping with Secrets*
**Sex has never been
so shamelessly gratifying....**

*Available wherever Harlequin books are sold.*

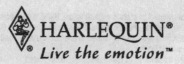

**HARLEQUIN®**
® *Live the emotion*™

www.eHarlequin.com                    HBSWS

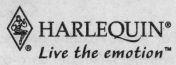